THE BACKSIDE OF THURSDAY

Raymond Kolcaba

RAYMOND KOLCABA

outskirts press

The Backside of Thursday

v4.0 r1.0

Outskirts Press, Inc.
http://www.outskirtspress.com

Paperback ISBN: 978-1-9772-1269-6

PRINTED IN THE UNITED STATES OF AMERICA

Thanks to H.P. and M.M.

1

THE DOG IN THE TREE

The big dame in my apartment kept telling me to eat my spinach. That lady cared more about my scrawny appearance than what brought her here. She had this little dog. It ran into the park. Everybody was walking the park looking for her dog. They were all wandering around calling, "Muffin, Muffin," in this high-pitched voice that you only hear when someone calls for a small dog. Then this little kid looked up and saw the dog— mutilated near the top of a tree. What a gruesome sight, and you couldn't even put a little sheet over it, you know, to mask the corpse. Gruesome sight.

The lady came to me because I'm a private investigator—Jack de Loosh™, PI. I told her, her name being Arbuckle, that her dog was found. It wasn't in good shape but that there was little I could do. But she kept harping on my eating habits. What did she know about my habits? I think she was projecting her weight problem onto me. I would look more oblong if I ate what she ate.

I knew that she wasn't going to pay me to eat, so I brought her back to the dog again and again. You know how it is. An old, very mature lady likes to break up her day talking to someone. When she runs out of doctors to talk to, she turns to a private eye. I have to admit, though, I don't get a lot of old ladies coming to my apartment to talk. I think she might've paid me if I just looked right. To look embarrassed over my eating habits.

These dog cases end up twisted. You don't know where they'll lead. I warned her that an investigation would cost a lot of money, maybe end up damaging innocent lives, and we probably wouldn't know what happened anyway. I was sarcastic. What do you think, the fire department mutilated the dog, climbed a ladder, and put it up in the tree? Do you think somebody kidnapped the dog, put it on an airplane, and dropped it on the tree? As we left it, Miss Arbuckle would work up a better menu for me, and I'd come up with some story about the dog.

2

ANDRE'S EMPORIUM

That old lady made me obsess about food. Most of my friends do that to me too. I made a beeline to the deli and scored a couple of candy bars and strong black coffee. Nothing like a breakfast of candy bars and black coffee. It's almost as good as beer and Wheaties. It wakes you up. Gets you ready for the day. You don't have to worry about eating for a while. Some days if I'm really lucky, I'd have a couple of crullers or even an elephant ear. Let's leave talk about food until later.

While chomping on my third candy bar, I entered Andre's Pet Grooming Emporium. Andre and I go back to the days when ballroom dancing meant something. Now it's all disco. Too hypnotic. Not intimate.

If anybody knew things about dog mutilation, it would be Andre. He gives them some strange cuts. The dogs are innocent. They don't know how bad they look. All the weirdoes who dress up dogs as cowboys, ballet dancers, and clowns show up here.

You've got the picture that Andre's seen it all. He has this big pompadour and some missing teeth in front, but he's a sweet guy and knows his stuff. "Hey Jock-O my boy," he said. He used to be a pirate. I'll bet that a lot of pirates retire and become pet groomers. That's why he doesn't get his teeth fixed.

It would spoil his look.

"Andre at work. What're you doing to that one? Getting him ready for a bike parade?"

"No, just cleaning him and making him look like this picture."

Some of these dog owners see some dog in a magazine groomed like Clark Gable, with his slick matted down hair, and ask Andre to oil up their dog that way.

The way that Andre perfumes the dogs, you have to light up a cigarette to mask the sweet sickening odor. I lit one up. Andre saw it coming. I blew smoke and asked,

"Did you hear about the mutilated toy dog in the tree?"

"Yeah Jock-O, a lot of owners are doubling down on their insurance."

"I'm working that case."

"Well the cops could care less. They look at it as an act of God or something. You would think God had better things to do than mutilate dogs and put them in trees."

"So, I won't bump into anyone else on the trail?"

"I don't know what a trail would look like. Who's on it? No idea. Unless it's some crazy religious cult."

"Yeah Andre. Nobody went up into the tree to mutilate the dog."

"Well I'm glad that you aren't letting it drop."

"Not me, my client needs closure. And somebody should find out what happened to her furry friend."

"Yep, it's good that somebody cares."

"It was a Havanese with a puppy cut. Did you do it?"

"Naw. Not my dog. When you're trimming the aim is to make it as cute as possible. The cuter the puppy cut, the bigger the tip."

These groomers try to make the mature, adult dogs look like cute baby dogs forever. Draw people in with the cuteness of babies. Pooches included. That's how Disney made his fortune. Making animated dwarfs and animals look like people babies. Cute. Cute. Cute.

I continued, "You know dog owners, especially the kind with toy dogs. Are there quirks I should be looking for?"

"They usually seem to have an obsession with food."

"That makes sense. My lady is rectangular, you know boxy, and she harped on my skinniness."

"They try to feed those little dogs like there's no tomorrow."

"I didn't hear that it was a fat mutilated Havanese."

"It's hard to tell because they're so fluffy."

"Proves that chubby is good. That's a help Andre. I'll look into the dog's weight and take it from there."

3

THE PET CEMETERY

There's no morgue for dogs. There's no oddball coroner in this story. But I didn't want to go back and ask Miss Arbuckle if her dog had a weight problem. Maybe it had a heart attack or something. That's why I was there in the dead of night at the pet cemetery with my shovel. I walked past tombstone after tombstone. You quickly walk by a lot of them because a lot of them are for tiny animals. From above, it's like a big train set with graves on it.

There were some statues of dogs with noble bearing, pointing or guarding something. Then there was this turtle. It was an imposing turtle. It made an impression. They couldn't give the turtle a noble bearing. Well, to be honest, I couldn't tell if it had a noble bearing. Reptiles are like that. No square-jawed clear-eyed turtles. Maybe in cartoons. Not in real life.

Ah! There was the Muffin plot. Bless her heart. The little angel. In that cute little grave. Next to her tiny stone. The stone read, "To my reason for living—Albion." Miss Arbuckle must've written that. She must've loved that dog. Most people don't get a tribute like that. I could tell Arbuckle was sentimental.

Next to Muffin's little plot was a gigantic plot with a massive stone on it. It was for an eagle. Next to it, there was this pedestal with a sculpture of a giant eagle. The stone said, "Alfie the Golden Eagle." I checked the date and it was the same as

Muffin's year. Alfie must've been buried right after Muffin. Who would keep a golden eagle as a pet anyway? I think you have to feed those things live food, at least some of the time. They probably don't have very good table manners.

I figured that parts of the dog were missing with the mutilation and all, and it had been down there for a while moldering. So, a quick look wouldn't tell me much about how chubby Muffin was. I planned to use science and weigh the remains. I brought my bathroom scale. I'd weigh myself. I'd hold the remains and weigh myself. I'd subtract the difference. Just as I struck the coffin, I saw some lights and heard some commotion. I scattered the dirt back, hid the shovel, and scurried to the road walking as if nothing was going on. You know, whistling Dixie. Yep, a friendly squad car was on me.

"Hey Lou. I think that guy is shamus Jack."

"You're right Pete."

"Yo Jack, what're you doing in this cemetery? What's that under your arm?"

"Is that you Lou? What're you doing in the grave yard?"

"What about you? Did you decide to leave your bathroom and weigh yourself in the cemetery at night?" Pete asked.

"Ha, Ha. I was taking the scale to Julie's so she could weigh in. She's going on a diet."

"Likely story. There's something going on here. Every time we bump into you Jack, there seems to be something strange going on. If we find there's more to this, we'll be back. You're not supposed to be in here after dark."

"I know to you cops everything looks funny. But if there's a scoop for you guys, I won't hold back. I'll be quick to let you in on it."

"What kind of scoop could it be Jack? The pooper kind? You get that one Lou? Ha. Ha. Hey look, the scale isn't concealed. Heh, heh. It doesn't look like a weapon. Hearty Har Har."

"You guys should be comedians. Why don't you go catch

some criminals?"

"You got any handy Jack?"

"I do have a weighty case guys! Real heavy."

"Let's get out of here Pete before his jokes put us to sleep."

4

JULIE AND THE SCALE

After the squad car drove off, I doubled back to the Muffin tomb, but darned it, I couldn't find the shovel. So, scale in hand, I headed over to Julie's. I hadn't eaten since breakfast. I usually forget to eat. I can usually hit up Julie for some snacks. She wondered where I'd been, and the scale under my arm couldn't be hidden. Right away she took offense. She honked like an offended swan. I tried to tell her about poor Muffin but she yelled and said that I was throwing hints. Really? Who'd bring a scale to his girlfriend's house to throw a hint? After her edge wore off, I scored some Pepsi and chips.

I told her the story about Arbuckle and Muffin and the tomb and Alfie the golden eagle. She thought it was the most cockeyed case she'd ever heard of. What did weighing the remains have to do with the mutilated dog in the tree? "You're trying to cover up your real motive in coming here with that scale." With emphasis on poor Muffin, I tried to have it all make sense and to save face by working up some yarn about that predator Alfie. It was an awkward silence when she challenged me. How do you get hot on the trail of a dead eagle? And then the doorbell rang.

There were old reliables Lou and Pete, those snooping John Law coppers. Lou was holding my shovel. Pete said I had a lot of explaining to do. He said that somebody had started to dig up the Muffin grave.

"You were the only one out there Jack." Lou said.

I told them that I was just passing through the cemetery when I saw them.

"Then whose shovel is this?" as Lou held the shovel out toward me.

"Not mine."

Pete didn't miss a thing. "If this was a criminal case, we'd have it finger printed, and guess what Jack? Your prints would be all over it."

"And what's with that scale? You'd said that you were taking it to Julie's."

And with that, Julie burst into tears and kicked us all out.

5

THE TORN SHADE

Outside I told the guys that they shouldn't have brought up the scale. Julie was very sensitive about her weight. Now she was full of storm clouds and hurt. She was disturbed and feeling bad about herself.

"You insensitive, hardened old jerks. Have some etiquette. Some feelings." I said.

I made them feel like heels and that changed the subject from the dig in the cemetery. After some practice you get good at changing the subject.

"I don't know Jack. For somebody with a 'sensitive' girlfriend, I've no idea why you'd walk a scale over to her house. I guess you were just looking for trouble." Lou said.

I moseyed back to my apartment to have a beer and go to bed. All the excitement left me frazzled. I have this darned torn shade on the window right above my bed. It seemed that just as I'd dozed off, the dawn's breaking through that window. The shaft of light caught me right on my head. Coming through where that lousy shade was torn. I rolled around for a while trying to avoid that shaft of light. I started thinking about going out to buy a new shade. That was it; I had to get up.

I started to think about my day. I want to tell you that I don't have much sentiment for dead animals. As a bottom line confession, I couldn't care less about Muffin and Alfie. What

I really needed was a good story to spin to Miss Arbuckle. My aim for the day was to come up with a story I could sell to Arbuckle and get paid. I thought that I should somehow try to tie in Alfie the eagle, add a little color to the story. Make her feel that I was really looking into things.

6

MY REPO PAST

Before we get too far ahead of things, I'd better fill you in on me and Julie. She isn't always kicking me out. We get along pretty well. We have an arrangement that goes back to my repo days. I was living in Hoboken working as a wheelman for a repo artist. I call him an artist because stealth and timing are everything repossessing cars. You nail a car in the wee hours while trouble sleeps. If my boss ran into trouble, like getting caught in the act, you needed a quick getaway. That was my job.

One night this guy got the drop on us and chased us with a gun. We got away but he started stalking us. This nice office worker at the business hid me out in her place. The stalking went on and on. If I was some big burly guy, he wouldn't have even started the stalking— the bully. That's how Julie and I got together. We kind of slid into this relationship. Don't get me wrong. She has it all. She's smart, pretty, and best of all, we get along. That wasn't easy when I was being stalked for weeks on end.

We decided to drop the repo business and move here to the Midwest. I'd learned a lot about people's habits and how the law worked. So, the move into private investigating was easy. Julie gave up on my business early on and took a steady job. My pay for being a PI was spotty. Even with big cases, the people didn't want to pay up. I heard one sob story after another or they just skipped out on me. I don't know how many liens I have on properties. I don't have the money to hire a collection agency to get my money. I have a season pass to Small Claims Court. I've been living hand to mouth for too long.

That was years ago. But Julie and I stayed an item. We've kept working on our arrangement over the years. Some time back we decided that our next step together depended on when my income stopped being spotty. I was waiting for some insurance company, you know with deep pockets, to give me a big contract. I also wanted to do a lot of side work for the cops. I know a lot of them, but they're slow in making offers. I'm still waiting for my chance. I can't afford an office so I work out of my apartment. Now we're caught up.

7

BIRDMAN FRITZ

My first instinct about the dog was that a predator did it. I needed to talk to people who knew about predators. I headed to the natural history museum to tap my buddy Birdman Fritz. I found Fritz in one of the enclosures doing who knows what to a buzzard. Not that what he was doing was too unusual. Don't get the wrong idea.

"Hey Birdman, how're the birdies?" I asked.

"We had a few get sick and die recently."

"You've got to stop feeding them junk food."

"Not me, the public sneaks in junk food and throws it into the cages. You can tell by the wrappers in there like Baby Ruth and Snickers."

"I should hang out in one of those cages. I like that stuff."

"Always on the make for food, huh Jack?"

"Right now, I'm working a case involving a golden eagle."

"Those are powerful birds Jack-man. It takes a lot to keep them healthy. Our eagle needs to exercise its wings to avoid muscle degeneration. We take ours to a field to let it stretch its wings. Now suppose that it spots a nice juicy chihuahua. Swoops before I can call it back. What then happens? You don't stick around to find out. You get your eagle back, leave the dog, and sneak over to the van."

"Well suppose Fritz, that a golden eagle got ahold of a toy

dog. What would it do with it?"

"It would grab it, fly to some high place, and tear it to shreds."

"Not bad, that's what happened to this toy dog I'm investigating. Torn to shreds up at the top of a tree."

"So you want to know if an eagle did it?"

"Yeah, especially a golden eagle."

"All you have to do is examine the remains and you'll know."

"Well, how can I tell?"

"Show me the remains and I'll give you a professional opinion."

"Good enough Fritz."

So, we agreed to meet after dark at the gate of the pet cemetery. The cops confiscated my shovel, so I had to go buy another one. I also bought a good flashlight. That's so Fritz could get a good look. I would give Muffin a good weighing. Somehow this case was coming along.

8

CHUBBY OR NOT?

After grabbing a Creamsicle, I headed to meet Birdman. He was already at the cemetery. He took the flashlight. I carried the scale and the shovel. We got to Muffin's grave and began digging. You know how it is when digging up a grave with someone. You can't stop talking.

"If the dog's dead, why does this lady want to know what killed it? Morbid curiosity?"

"I don't care Fritz, she's paying me."

We pulled up the little vault and opened the coffin; Fritz shined the light and said,

"There are pieces of it missing. Where's the head?"

"It's hard to tell that it was a dog. Don't all of those dogs look chubby being a puff ball of fur?"

"Sure, you don't know what you've got until you shave them. Why did you want to know whether it was chubby?"

"That says something about their owners. Someone wouldn't dognap it unless it was chubby."

"Are you saying that someone dognapped it?"

"I don't know. That's why we're here."

"But who would dognap it, mutilate it, and then throw it up in a tree?"

"It would take some mighty weird character. Well Fritz, did an eagle do it?"

"I can't tell from all the white fur and gray meat. The remains are in too bad a shape."

I saw that weighing the dog wouldn't tell us much. It was hard to tell how much of the dog was there.

Fritz then looked over at the Alfie tomb.

"You were right Jack-man. Somebody did love that eagle. They put a fortune into that eagle sculpture."

I said maybe it's an X marks the spot kind of thing. Suppose somebody wanted to bury some loot until they got out of prison when an old man. They would want to make it easy to find.

"Are you saying that that's no eagle lover?"

"Just say'in."

"That would make sense if the eagle statue wasn't such a target for thieves."

"Yeah, it won't last long in this cemetery."

We then dug up Alfie. When we opened the lid, our eyes got big. Wow! There was Alfie fully intact. Lying on his back. His wings were flat against his sides. Like he was asleep. His feet were straight up in the air. That signaled, "dead bird." Fritz told me about that signal. Eagles don't sleep on their backs. I guess I knew that already. Maybe when in eternal rest, they sleep on their backs. Some miserable undertaker must have given the eagle that pose to make the owner happy.

Fritz said that Alfie didn't meet the same fate as Muffin. I pointed out that we didn't know where Alfie was found.

Fritz said, "I don't mean he was mutilated and up in a tree. I mean that he wasn't mutilated."

"Wow, he almost looks alive."

"Except he's on his back with his feet in the air."

We returned the graves to normal as best as we could. We had no new ideas, so we took our gear and headed to the road.

9

SWEATING US

Just as we turned onto the road, all those bright lights were shining in our eyes. The cavalry had arrived. Those friendly cops with nothing better to do. Lou took the lead.

"Hello boys. I see that you have the scale and a shovel this time."

"Are you guys headed over to Julie's because it would now take two of you to weigh her?" Pete asked.

"Yeah, it'd take two of um. Julie would be kicking and screaming not wanting to get on that scale."

"Very funny. Can the insults guys. We don't need to insult you. You insult yourselves when you look in a mirror. The shock every morning should've made your hearts give out years ago."

Fritz tried to bring down our emotions. "Slow down guys. What is the problem?"

The boys started their interrogation. "Well, what about the shovel?"

"You accused me of having a shovel last time Pete. Today when I set out with my scale, I thought, 'Hmm. If I run into the boys, I had better bring a shovel. To make the boys happy.'"

"Then if you got caught there'd be two of you to concoct a tall tale." Lou cracked.

"All I can give you guys is the swear-on-the-Bible truth."

"Jack, you wouldn't know truth if the sky opened up and God pointed and said, 'here is the truth.'"

"You cops need some community training, you know, to improve community relations."

"We love the community but you guys aren't part of it. And Fritz, why do you hang out with this guy? Oh, I know, he needs someone with a brain to help him, but you don't have to go along with him when he doesn't use his brain."

Fritz started into a cover story. I hadn't the foggiest idea where he was going with the owl business. He said we were in the cemetery studying owls.

The boys looked at each other in wonder, wondering where that one came from. Pete asked if we're going to kill owls, weigh them, and then bury them.

Fritz went on, "No, small dead pets in the area could be the work of owls."

"Oh yeah. what about the scale?" Lou asked.

Fritz explained that if we found dead prey, we would need to weigh it. We were looking for buried owl prey. You know, some good Samaritan may have been burying owl prey in the cemetery. Pete asked if we'd found any. Fritz said, "In the negative, Captain."

The boys sensed we were giving them the run around. and that we thought they were born yesterday. Well, if you asked me, I would say yesterday was too far back.

"Last time shamus Jack, you started to dig in the Muffin grave. You got some kind of an obsession with that poor little dog?" Pete asked.

"It's all about research guys. We're just starting our research."

Lou said that what we're doing was illegal. I said that the owner sent us here. Lou asked for the owner's name and that they would check out my story. At this point I swallowed hard. Arbuckle wouldn't like our digging up Muffin.

"Hey you guys, give us some time. The owner is in grief.

The poor lady wanted to know what happened to her dog. After we find out, you can ask her what you want."

Pete said, "I know you Jack. You just want to be paid before she learns of the grave robbing."

I tried to put them on the spot that if they don't care about the owner, I do. I'm more sensitive.

Lou quipped, "You sugar-junky shamus. You're sensitive all right."

Fritz was really good at false sincerity. He reeked of it. "Nobody can bring back Muffin. The only person to be hurt by all of this is the dog's owner."

"Jack can be hurt. Right Pete? Break some laws and we'll go after you. We'll see you later. You better watch out Jack."

The cops finally moved on. It was a relief. I was sweating hard. It was like I was under the bright lights at the station. I never liked being interrogated. Well, the more we said, the more convoluted our story. It was like the air going out of a balloon. Our balloon was just about flat. Fritz and I headed to the soda shop for a little late-night snack. I had a chocolate raspberry soda. Nothing like a soda to put you to sleep. What was my next step? I'd no idea. Maybe tomorrow something would come to me.

10

JUNGLE TOM

At the break of dawn, the phone rang hard and it was a disturbed Miss Arbuckle. The boys in blue must've gone to the cemetery and asked for the name of the owner of the Muffin plot. They spilled the beans. Police-community relations were building in my ears. And oh was she letting me have it. She was so worked up that I put the phone on the table to wait for the shouting to stop. That woman knows how to cry. And really out loud.

First, it was, "How could you be so ….," "Whoever heard of such disrespect for the dead." "My poor little dog didn't deserve….," and the best one, "You don't care about my feelings." After that, she lit into my eating habits again and how only such a malnourished man could be so twisted. With me, these things always come back to food. She then said that she wanted to meet so we could end this thing and that I should go on to eat better and improve my health. Fine with me so long as I was paid.

I was glad that I didn't think so badly of myself. That constant shouting can get to you after a while. My health was kind of good. But what she said did stress me out. I needed a couple of cigarettes and a cup of strong black coffee to level off. On the way to the coffee shop I picked up a piece of chocolate cake for breakfast. Overnight I decided that the eagle and dog deaths were unrelated. They just occurred around the same time. What could have killed Muffin? I was still thinking about predators. I decided to go to the zoo to visit my buddy— Jungle Tom.

Now Tom took a number of trips to Africa and South America to collect animals for the zoo. He might have some ideas about the mutilation. I caught up with him hosing down the gorilla exhibit. After a night of gorillas peeing, the place reeked of gorilla pee. For some reason Tom doesn't want to use air fresheners to sweeten the air. You know, give the gorilla enclosure a nice pine scent. Zoo-keepers always want to make sure that we the public know the gorilla smell. That way if you're, say, shopping at Macy's and you smell the gorilla smell, you know to be alert, to watch out for a gorilla.

Now Tom had these tall rubber boots, a raincoat, and a mask over his face. The gorilla probably thought he was a space alien. But zoos don't care what animals think. They just try to keep them alive and breed them. You should see what these big guys eat and how much. In the morning, you know after nature calls, what a mess. But Jungle Tom was happy as an oyster on a reef. The way some people get their jollies mystifies me.

Over the sound of the hose gushing water, I said loudly, "Hey Tom."

He shouted back, "Hi Jack-son. You on another case?"

"You got that right Tom."

"What did some animal do that brings you in?"

He turned off the hose and walked over.

"I have some suspicions about the death of a dog."

"Hey Jack-son, not to be offensive or anything, you look bad. Haven't you been eating? You should eat a vegetarian diet like this gorilla. I'll give you a cage right next door. I'll feed you gorilla food until you look as good as that gorilla! Yuk! Yuk!"

I tried to catch him off guard. "If I were living in one of these cages, I'd never eat because of the stench." That stopped him in his tracks.

I told him the story of Muffin and asked him if there was an animal that could do such a thing. He put on a serious look and began lisping an answer. He always lisped when he wanted to sound important like he's the inside dopester. Like he's letting you in on something. Anyway, he said it looked like the work of a cat. Well I had seen a lot of cats in the neighborhood and none of them could take a dog to the top of a tree and mutilate it.

Tom lisped, "You've got to think outside of the box."

I didn't know I was thinking inside a box. Whoever says that doesn't come up with a box. They don't know what box they're talking about. Ok, Ok, I took it as a challenge and put-down. I didn't want him to think outside the box. I wanted to know what he knew. You can tell that Tom knows how to push my buttons. He doesn't even know he's pushing them. Finally Tom said that the one cat capable of doing that to a dog was a leopard. He said that leopards live in jungles and climb trees. They kill prey and then take it up in a tree to eat it. Whatever they can't eat, they store high in a tree so other animals can't get to it. They return later for a snack. I told Tom that the attack occurred in a city park. He said that there were exotic animal collectors that could lose their animal for a time and then recapture it before the public knew what happened.

It did seem that some exotic animal collectors had to sneak around the law. I could just see Lou and Pete on the trail of a leopard. Those guys are really great animal trackers. They'd follow the animal in their squad car. Ha Ha. Follow some leopard in a nice leisurely way? Too much effort. No, they would rather go after low hanging fruit like me in the pet cemetery with my scale.

How could I look into what Tom said? He told me that animal collectors bought carnivore meat from a wholesaler. Some meat dealers specialized in horsemeat and other cuts that people don't like. I set out for the meat place.

11

THE MEAT WAREHOUSE

I entered the warehouse through the loading dock. There was a guy with a dolly, loading cartons of meat onto a truck. I asked for the salesman. He said, "Go see Milo in the back." You couldn't miss Milo. He filled a doorway and kind of looked like a bulldog. He wore this white coat. Why do meat people wear white coats? They always get them full of blood and Milo's coat was no exception. You'd think they wouldn't get that much blood on them after they got good at butchering. I guess it doesn't work that way. Maybe they liked the blood on their coats. It looked like they've been working.

I introduced myself as Heintz Roldo animal collector. I told him that I was branching out into jungle cats. I wondered if he could give me some tips. He said that he didn't know much about how to keep these cats, but he knew exactly what they should eat. He said that such animals required a lot of supplements but their basic diet is meat. He said that this was his specialty. I said, "I guess I'm in the right place." He nodded. I was glad we got that established.

After talking about the pros and cons of cow versus horsemeat, I interrupted him and asked if there was a collector in the area who could give me some advice. He looked in his Rolodex and came up with some names. I asked if any had a leopard. He said the third one, the James guy, Bartemus

James. He had a leopard and was always talking about it. I had my lead.

My appetite was ruined by the zoo stench and bloody clothing, so I picked up some fries from a street vendor. I smothered them with ketchup. I was on my way to Miss Arbuckle's apartment. I dreaded talking to her. I decided that whatever I had to put up with, I wouldn't leave until I got her to write a check. I figured if I appealed to the fact that I was short of money and didn't have enough money for food, she would cave in and help me out. Save me from starvation. Miss Arbuckle, save me, please.

12

THE SAGGING FLYING SAUCER

When I knocked on her door, I heard this, "Go away. 'Sob, sob.' I am not ready to face this abuse. You fiendish monster. 'Sob, sob.'"

After some time talking through the door, I think she got tired of the display. I wheedled my way in with a promise of news about Muffin. She was some sight— looking very large and rectangular, heaving up and down with kerchief in hand. I don't know what the boys in blue told her to make her so crazy. I stuck with it and waited for the heaving to stop.

She had these thick drapes over everything that could hold a drape. Right on the mantle was a large happy picture of Muffin. What was odd was that there were no pictures of anyone else. It was as if she plopped down from outer space into this draped cave. And it was dustier than my place. I usually don't notice dust. Here I moved a little and dust flew. Now that's dusty when you move around a little and kick up dust.

The flying saucer that brought her here probably sagged in the middle. You know, where her seat was. She made the space trip alone to spare other travelers all of the hysterics. Maybe she saved her pent-up emotion from hundreds of years of space travel just for me.

She finally became calm enough to say, "I was told that there were two of you grave robbers."

"I was there with my adviser Birdman who knows a lot about birds."

"Muffin isn't a bird."

I pointed to her picture of Muffin and said, "I can tell that from her picture, that she's not a bird. We thought that maybe she was killed by a golden eagle."

"Why would an eagle hurt my little dog? She got along with everybody."

I then explained how eagles prey on small animals. They get hungry for food and then they can't help themselves. I added some color to the story a bit by pointing out that dogs put up a good fight and ruffle some feathers.

"Were there feathers in Muffin's coffin?"

"No, after looking at Muffin, we decided that it wasn't an eagle that killed her."

"When you opened the coffin, how did my little Muffin look?"

At this point I didn't want to tell her that she didn't have a head and that we couldn't tell if she looked chubby.

I said, "She looked dignified in that little coffin."

"Did the mortician make her look good? Was she properly dressed?"

Wow! She thought they embalmed her or something and put her in a wedding dress.

"All I'll say is that she had regal bearing. You would have been proud."

"She did stand out as more dignified than other dogs."

"We carefully put back the lid, lowered her down, and said a few words."

With that she began to cry again.

I explained that I knew the police were only doing their job. I said that I told the police that I didn't want to upset her and ask for an exhumation. I told her that I was sorry that they made me seem like a grave robber or worse.

She said, "You did the best you could."

"I'll continue looking for the killer, but I need a little money for food."

"You seem skinnier than before. You had better eat. I'll make you some healthy food."

I said, "Ur, I have to go meet my lady friend, but if I could have an advance, that'd tide me over."

She said, "I'll write you a nice check."

I thought I was home free. She wrote the check and sealed it in an envelope. When I got outside, I opened the envelope and my eyes bugged out. The check was for ten dollars! That wasn't enough for a good snack.

Well, I didn't want to go back and ask for more. I suspected that this lady was sharper than I thought. After the waterworks, she got the information she wanted, and when I tried to make her feel sorry for me, she was all heart about my not eating. But what about helping me? Next time, I thought, I had to leave with something to show for it.

13

JULIE'S DIET

It was getting late so I decided to head over to Julie's to hit her up for something to eat. The leopard business could wait til tomorrow. Julie was in a good mood and glad to see me. Right away I knew something was up. She smiled and broke the news. She's going on a diet and that I should bring the scale back so she could weigh in. Cold chills ran up my spine. My ears were lit. I turned pale. Well, paler than before. What a trap.

Every time she went on a diet, I ended up being the whipping boy. No matter what I said now, weeks of conflict were coming. Form the battle lines. Watch out.

What could I do? I had to bring the scale back. Maybe I could give some lame excuse like the boys in blue confiscated it for evidence? Or, I broke it? No chance of that.

The way it usually goes, she's delighted to go on a diet. Once the diet doesn't work so well, she begins telling me that I'm too thin. I don't look healthy. It looks like I'm not taking care of myself. What she means but doesn't say is that she wouldn't look overweight standing next to a bulked-up version of me. I usually tell her that she looks healthy. Why tamper with a good thing? She then says that I don't care about how she looks.

I once tried telling her that she was a pound or two over weight. Shed those pounds and she would be perfect. She accused me of not being honest with her and that if I really cared I would help her. I tried agreeing with her every opinion, nodding my head like a bobble-head doll. After a while she caught on and said something negative. "You don't want me to look good." When I nodded like a machine, nod, nod, nod, she caught me.

She knew what body image she wanted. I'd be happy if she'd be happy. She didn't believe me. She'd then accuse me of wanting to dump her. Some skinny girl would come along and I'd be gone. I never said that skinny girls looked good. What was I thinking in bringing that damn scale to her place?

I said to her that I'd help her with her diet, but it'd create a problem with her plate being empty and my plate full of food. What'd she say when her plate had two string beans on it while mine was loaded up with a big pile of spaghetti? Then, crash, she had a strategy. She said that she wanted me to eat a big dinner before I got to her place. After I arrived, I'd have dinner the same as hers. She'd eat a measly morsel and I'd get a measly morsel too. Criminy, I couldn't just pop in for some carbs to tide me over.

The aim of my big dinner was to fatten me up. She also wanted me to weigh in with her. That was a first. She wanted me to agree that she'd lose as many pounds as I'd gain. Boy, she was going all out trying to blow up our arrangement. All of this worry made me hungry. We ordered a pizza and popped open a couple of Cokes. I told her all about the stench at the zoo, the meat warehouse, and all of Arbuckle's sopping drama. She didn't eat much pizza.

I stayed over at her place. I thought I'd better take advantage of her good feelings before our relationship turned into a daily struggle. Honestly, I'd never been able to gain weight. Since I was a little kid, even around Easter time with all of the chocolate eggs and marshmallow peeps, my weight didn't budge. If she lost more than I gained, she would show me up. In a way I didn't care. Gaining weight wasn't my idea. I knew I wasn't good at it.

14

A COMMUTING LEOPARD?

Julie had a good idea that when I visited Bartemus James I should ask him about big cat activity in the area. You know, we collectors of exotic animals often get a bad rap when others are to blame. Appeal to his group loyalty. He lived outside of town, and as I drove along, I began thinking that his leopard had quite a commute to the park. Only to find that little dog?

There was a high, electrified fence and a gate with a buzzer. When he came to the door, he didn't look too tied into the present. He had a distant look like a cat has when it isn't feeding. He seemed cat-like. They say people are imitative. They behave like their animals. So, people who keep pigs oink around, root around, aren't clean. That's a humorous example. There are better ones but I can't think of one offhand. We always want pets to be just like us but we turn out being more like them.

I guess that's true with dogs but it doesn't seem to work with turtles. Once in elementary school there was a kid who didn't express himself much. I never thought then it might've been because he had this sizable turtle. Come to think of it, he did slow down when it got cold outside. He. He.

Bartemus was friendly enough. He liked answering questions. You know these exotic animal people always have interesting stories to tell. A lot them are about doing the animal count in the morning only to find you're short some animals. Somehow, they think that they are going to have their own Garden of Eden. Some animals tear other animals apart. That's their instinct. It's their nature. I once heard that cheetahs always sever the spinal cords of prey at the same vertebra, the seventh or something. After bitten, the prey animal tries to run but its rear legs are detached from its brain. Anyway, that's too gruesome.

I was interested in leopards, so I maneuvered Bartemus into talking about his leopard. They do have the behavior that Jungle Tom told me about. They carry dead prey into a tree, feed, and leave the rest for later. I also learned that leopards, especially wild ones, are very expensive and that some laws have to be broken to bring one from the wild. I thanked Bartemus for his help and said I'd keep in touch so he could give more advice about how my leopard-keeping was going, wink, wink.

On the trip back, I mulled over all the information I had. The leopard idea seemed like a dead end. One, you need a leopard. For what I could tell, none were anywhere around the park. Two, James' house was too far. Someone would've spotted the leopard before it would've killed poor Muffin. Three, no self-respecting leopard would nail a little dog. It was too small. An appetizer, maybe. A main course, no way. Four, why would it leave anything? Unless it was some leopard trying to lose weight and only eating a very small meal. I shouldn't have brought Julie into this, but I couldn't get the diet thing out of my head. A leopard might figure into the story, but I was far from being convinced.

15

A THERAPY DOG

I stopped at Ice Cream Island and had a double-decker cone for lunch. I had it dipped in chocolate and sprinkled some nuts on it. Now there's a high calorie meal. Julie said she wanted to fatten me up. Why didn't she feed me like that. Why didn't she give me the high calorie food that she eats? I always end up with popcorn and diet pop or those snowballs made of coconut and marshmallow— you know, the pink and white ones. I have to admit, though, that at times she tried to cook a regular dinner and that I didn't finish my plate. I started out eating away. I then slowly tapered off. My appetite slowly vanished. Pretty soon I had trouble lifting the fork.

Well, she loads the food onto her plate. In order not to look like an overeater, to put it politely, she heaps even more on my plate. What am I supposed to do with all that food? I can't sneak it to the dog. She doesn't have a dog. She always brings it up that I eat like a church mouse. If I was a mouse, I wouldn't live in a church—you hear all of that praying hour after hour but there's no food. It doesn't help if you're a mouse praying for food. There's nobody upstairs to answer mouse prayers.

As I entered the city, I had a brilliant idea. Maybe, Arbuckle had enemies. I'd been assuming that some animal got the dog. Anyone who didn't like Arbuckle and wanted to harm her, knew how much she cared about that little dog. So, we entered the dirty trick phase of the investigation. For what I knew, Arbuckle had no friends and probably no enemies. Her apartment gave no clues about any social contacts. I needed to visit her and ask about enemies.

When I arrived at her apartment, she again tore into my diet. I asked her whether she was following me around watching what I ate. She said that I looked worse than the last time she saw me. She said I was one step away from the grave. Why was she so worried? Then she wouldn't have to pay me.

I decided to lay off the sarcasm. I mentioned that I was working hard. I told her my girlfriend challenged me to gain weight as she lost weight. She said that having someone support you is very helpful. I didn't offer the same challenge to her. Maybe I should have brought up her weight and vow to support her in losing a few pounds. I didn't bring up the paltry ten dollars she paid me last time. Maybe I should have said I would bring the scale over here. You know, threaten her a little.

I thought I would ease into the enemies thing, so I asked where she got Muffin. She teared up saying Muffin was a therapy dog. She'd been in an institution and it had this bring-in-the-therapy-dogs-one-day-a-week program. She said that the social worker saw that a bond formed between her and Muffin. When she was discharged, they let her keep the dog. It occurred to me that the dog was a reason why she recovered. The stay in the institution made sense because of her empty apartment and all of the thick curtains.

"Miss Arbuckle, in the institution did you and Muffin have any enemies?" She tried but couldn't answer that question. I asked the usual follow up, "Did anyone wish to do either of you harm?" I couldn't imagine that someone would so hate the dog that they'd wait until the dog was alone in the park before cutting off its head, mangling it, and putting it up in the tree. She replied that Muffin was much loved by everyone. "You were given Muffin to take home. Did you detect envy? Did others want Muffin for themselves?"

Miss Arbuckle didn't think so. She began to realize that other patients may have missed the dog when she took it away. She said she'd think about it. This line of questioning seemed stretched, but what about this case had been normal? She then said that Muffin had many admirers.

"Were any admirers about of her build and stature?" So as not to anger her, I asked if the admirer liked chubby dogs. She then said that they were the best and many people in the institution thought so too.

My head swam. I began putting the pieces together. Some other oblong admirer was into chubby toy dogs. When the dog was in the park, out popped the big lady, grabbed the dog, and checked it out to see if it was chubby behind that bushy coat. Once she found it wasn't, she or an accomplice, did the unthinkable. Ok, that is how the dirty deed might have been done. The problem was that Fritz and I in the pet cemetery couldn't tell if the dog was chubby.

I asked Arbuckle if she could give me the name of the chief rival. She said it was Fanny Blockman. I told her I'd look into that angle. Then she started in on my weight again. She asked what I had eaten today, and I wouldn't tell her. I said coyly that I spent the whole ten dollars on breakfast. I didn't know where my lunch would come from. Hint. Hint. She said she'd better write me another check. Once again, she put it into an envelope and sealed it before I could see the amount. When I got outside, I opened it. It was for only five dollars! What was that woman thinking?

16

A PHOTO OF DINNER

I was about to set out for Julie's. I remembered that I had to bring the scale. There was a remote chance that Julie would start that crazy diet when I arrived. I did some preparation at my favorite candy store. A couple of long strands of black licorice would put me right. I didn't want to be shocked with that single morsel on my plate, with my eyes bugging out, gasping for air. I probably would have trouble finding the small thing on the vastness of the plate. My attitude was lousy. Once again when walking toward Julie's, the boys in blue pulled alongside of me. As usual, Lou took the lead.

"Hey shamus Jack, you are taking your life in your hands taking that scale anywhere near Julie's."

Pete added, "Yeah, he's a glutton for punishment."

I told the wise guys, I'd weight them in. Then they would have to lose those bay windows.

"Does the chief require you to be able to run ten yards? You guys would have to be in training for six months to do it. Look at those slush guts. You couldn't catch anything moving except a rolling donut."

I think I managed to get them to take offense. That was a rare moment. They seemed peeved and drove off.

When I reached Julie's, she was beaming again. That's the signal that the trouble was going to start. She said, "Before we do anything, let's weigh in." And in this corner at 110 pounds we have Jack. And in that corner at 145 pounds we have Julie. I never gave a damn about my weight but it always was a good conversation starter. Anyway, Julie had a candle on the table, tablecloth and all, with two big plates and a bite on each plate. She said, "Let's sit down to dinner." Dinner? A termite eats more than that.

Anyway, she thought I'd had my big meal before I arrived. She asked me what I had for dinner. I hemmed and hawed, so she thought something was up. Then she saw the black licorice on the corners of my mouth. As I talked, she peered into my mouth— black teeth, black tongue. She accused me of not being sincere and not wanting to help her. I told her I thought we'd start the new plan after the weigh-in and that I didn't think it'd be the same night. After all, what's the rush? She didn't buy it.

To make matters worse, she had one of her brilliant ideas. I should take a picture of my big dinner and bring it when I came over. That way she'd know I was keeping my end of the bargain. What bargain? I didn't make a bargain. I enjoyed raiding Julie's snacks and making a dinner of it. Those days were over. I needed a better plan— one that would keep her happy and give me a break.

After dinner we broke open some diet pop and talked about the day. If there's anything I hate, it's diet pop They strip all of taste and wholesome ingredients from regular pop and sell you what's left. You know, they leave the artificial coloring and carbonated water. What happened to the real ingredient? Where's the real food? Where's the sugar?

I told her about my visit with Arbuckle. She became sad when she realized that the little dog was Arbuckle's ticket out of the institution. The little dog was all that she had. It's a story about how much trouble life can be. Along comes the toy dog that accepts you. Meaning comes into your life.

I left the scale at Julie's and tried to figure how I could put my thumb on it for the next weigh-in. I could get some lead fishing sinkers and put them in my pockets. The trouble was it'd take a lot of them to make the scale budge. I didn't want to make it seem that I could gain weight faster than she could lose it. She had to think that I would always be just a little behind her. The idea was to aim to have domestic tranquility and avoid domestic combat.

17

FORAGING AT STAN'S

The next morning the sun was blaring through that damn rip in my shade. That big shaft of light always landed right on my head. My eyelids turned bright red. I tried to roll over. I pulled up the covers. I knew I was trapped in that position. If I moved the wrong way, red eye lids again. All of this took so much figuring and effort that I had to get up. I thought about getting up before sunrise just to avoid this sorry routine. Of course, I hadn't. Just thinkin'. Maybe tomorrow.

So, I rose but didn't shine. I scrounged around the apartment for something to eat. There was a half-eaten sub sandwich. I only ate half at the time because I didn't like it. I moved on. There were a few soggy chips left in a bag. Not too appetizing. I had to enter the food chamber. People lose food that gets pushed into the back of a fridge. They discover it some months later. It always amazes me the things I tried to eat but didn't quite finish. I don't know why I tried to save the rest of it. It looks less appetizing over time. That's probably why it gets pushed way back there in the fridge. That's not really funny. I shouldn't romanticize the backs of refrigerators.

The back of my refrigerator was jammed with stuff. Somebody told me you wouldn't want to take a direct look back there. It might just look back at you. I heard that somewhere. After hearing it, I didn't want to look directly back there either.

It's just a superstition. There was probably genuine evolution going on in the back of that fridge. I've spent months trying not to disturb that evolution.

Since the front of the refrigerator was empty, I shut the door and took my foraging into Stan's apartment. He lived below me. Whenever I showed up at Stan's, he'd stand in the arch between his dining room and kitchen with his arms stretched. He wouldn't talk about this stance. It was sort of like the stance of a basketball player on defense. It was automatic when he saw me.

"Hidie ho Stan, good to see you." He wasn't fooled. I'd done a raid earlier in the week. As I walked in, he quickly stepped to his defensive position at the arch. The guy was treating me like a mooch. I once bought him a corn dog, but he always forgets that. With him in the arch, the rest of his place was fair game. His eyes were darting around the room looking for any food he might have mistakenly left out. I spied a few of those rancid peanuts that he always kept by his sofa in a bowl just in case company arrived. You have to make sure company doesn't come back.

Then what to my wandering eyes should appear but a four-pack of chocolate covered cherries. I pretended not to see them and just casually drifted over to them. When he saw my target, he broke for the box and said, "Would you like to have a chocolate?"

"If you insist Stan. You know I haven't had breakfast and thought we'd have it together."

"Really Jack? Are you buying?"

"I'm working on this big case about a little dog and I haven't been paid yet. You get this one, and I'll pick up the next one."

He said, "Sorry Jack, I have to run. I have to meet Gloria down town."

In leaving Stan's, I realized that my skill level had dropped. I couldn't count on my hunting skills. How could I survive in the apartment building jungle? I moved onto the food market for the free-sample harvest. I passed through the fruits. I don't like fruit. I grabbed a couple of those bits of sausage with toothpicks in them and some greasy crackers. Not bad. I ended with a hand full of candy— mostly jelly beans. The coffee bar offered a damn little cup of free coffee— single sip size. I moved on to tracking down Fanny Blockman.

18

THE DOG PACK

I went to Elysian Fields to make a start. The lady at the desk was very helpful. Fanny was still a resident. When I went to her room, it surprised me how much she looked like Arbuckle. She was sitting in a chair watching morning TV. I noticed a cane next to the chair. I introduced myself and asked her how she liked Elysian Fields. She was slow of speech, so it took a while to get responses. I asked her about the pet program and whether she liked little dogs.

Her face lit up. She emphasized the charm of the little chubby ones with bushy coats. I asked her if these days she had a favorite. She said that many were darling but, in the past, there were better dogs. Her favorite was the dog called Lily. To her Lily was the be all and end all of cuties. She said the eyes of that dog would melt your soul. Then one day a terrible thing happened. Someone let in a pack of dogs that attacked Lily. Lily was never the same and died the next month.

I asked if there were other wonderful dogs. She said that the little gal Muffin stood out. I asked what happened to Muffin. She said that someone gave Muffin to a resident that was about to be discharged. It broke her heart. And the big lady that got the dog was the one who let in the pack of dogs that killed Lily. Wow! There you have it. She had a motive to get even. The big lady must be Albion Arbuckle. But why would

Fanny kill Muffin? The dognapping motive seemed more likely.

As I drove away from Elysian Fields, I put it together that the lady with a cane couldn't catch Muffin, let alone mutilate her and get her into a tree. She moved in slow motion. She had to have a van take her anywhere. Van drivers always hang around close by. Fanny didn't have the power to do it or the opportunity. She might figure into a bigger picture though. Maybe part of a conspiracy. How was she connected to the fate of Muffin?

19

MUFFIN'S TREE

I got back to town and went to the scene of the killing. I wandered the park. I realized that a little dog could easily get lost in that big park. Easily fall victim to someone or something. From a picture, I found the tree where Muffin's body was found. How in the world could what was left of her end up, all the way up there? A large patch of grass was close by. I sat on a park bench to take a careful look at the scene.

Along came Jungle Tom. He was on his lunch break. He sat down with his brown bag. Tom still reeked from zoo smells. I bet his nose no longer told him how awful he smelled. It kind of made me sick watching him eat a blood baloney sandwich. I was starving but he curbed my appetite. I should have sent Julie to meet him for lunch. She wouldn't have to worry about adding calories. Just looking at any lunch would make her sick. Whew!

I told Tom what I was doing there. I described the scene that awful day when the kid saw Muffin in the tree. We were talking about the problem when all of a sudden, we could hardly hear each other talk. This industrial sized lawn mower came up. We had to stop talking. The mowing lasted only a few seconds. The thing had a wide cutting head and traveled a couple miles an hour.

Tom looked at me and said, "If something gets under that

lawn mower, mash, mash, it's gonna be mutilated." I had the same thought. Little Muffin, though, wouldn't be so stupid as to run in front of that big loud thing. She would have run and hid. And there was no way the mower could've shot the dog up there into the tree.

Tom offered me his apple. It was nice of him but I said that I was having appetite problems. Now if it were a big candy-apple— that would be different. All nice candy, shiny, and red— like a Corvette or something. Then I would've had my appetite back.

20

CHERUB DOGS

After Tom left, I tried to cancel the smell of gorilla urine with a couple of cigarettes. Ah, wholesome nicotine! As I passed a food vendor, I decided to have lunch, so I bought a cotton candy. That would tide me over until I made an appearance at Julie's. She wanted some kind of picture of my big dinner. I had to figure a way to fake it. As I was thinking of food, I got this vision of a package of sugar wafers. I headed for my food market the Seven Eleven. The wafers picked me up.

I decided to head back to Miss Arbuckle's. Maybe I could hit her up for more money. Maybe I could carry on a bit about how hungry I was. Maybe I could faint. Maybe I could give her a bill for work completed up to this point. That's it. Bill her. Even if she didn't come up with the money, it would be right there on paper what she owed me. It made no sense that she wanted to fatten me up but didn't care I'd no money for food. Maybe she didn't believe me. Maybe she thought I wouldn't buy food, take the money and have a wild time, gamble it away or something. I didn't know what to think.

One detail could be wrapped up. Fanny said that a big lady let in the pack of dogs that killed Lily. I could make sure that it was Arbuckle. I don't have the foggiest idea why Arbuckle would let in the pack of dogs. Or why anybody would let in a pack of dogs. I could see that Fanny might be out to even the score. I could firm up Fanny's motive. I had to figure out how to approach Arbuckle on the subject. She wouldn't own up to such an act. She probably would have a lot to say about that day. I could get a backgrounder on that day.

What did Miss Arbuckle do all day in that apartment? She didn't seem to have a TV. The thick drapes kept out most of the light. When I arrived, I said that I had an item of business. I took out my handy dandy pad of bills, and gave her a bill for $700 plus expenses.

"Just look at you, so thin. As thin as a toothpick," she said. "Your color isn't good. You're pale. Do you have a girl friend? She mustn't be taking very good care of you."

I said, "One problem I have is not enough money for food. Paying the bill would help me buy food." Was that direct enough or what?

"Don't worry about the bill. I will make you a nice sandwich."

Crap. I didn't want to be paid in food. Most of the stuff she'd fix would make me quiver. You know, give me the shakes. I explained to her that I was saving my appetite for dinner at Julie's.

"Oh, then you don't need money for food right now?"

"Well, it would help to have some pocket money, a few coins to jingle." I shouldn't have put it that way. It might've given her the idea to empty her change purse into my hand. That lady was a sharpie.

"Don't worry, I'll write you a check."

I explained how I was still losing weight from the last check she wrote. The idea was to prime the pump. Encourage her to put a nice big number on the check.

"You strike me as a loner. It's hard to be alone in the world. That's why you're so thin. How do you expect to do good work when you're hungry? Let me fix you a sandwich."

We rode that one around for a while. She wasn't going to budge. I didn't want to threaten to quit. This was my only job. I thought I would bring up food from another angle.

"What do you eat Miss Arbuckle?"

She said, "I get meals from the county. They usually are pasta or chicken or lunch meat."

"I thought you cooked big solid dinners."

She said those days were long past. She admitted having a sweet tooth. That was my opening.

"Do you have a piece of cake?"

"Sure Mr. de Loosher."

So, she "cooked" me a piece of cake. In the middle of the cake, I told her I visited Fanny Blockman at Elysian Fields. She was curious what I found out. I started into what happened.

"Fanny said there was a terrible accident. A pack of dogs was let in the door, and it killed her toy dog."

"Oh my, that was a terrifying day. The pack was going after any little dog. I hid Muffin to save her."

"Do you know how the dogs got in and where they came from?"

"Rumor had it that a lady with a well-established figure accidently opened the door. The dogs were roaming the grounds of the place."

"Did the lady with the big figure admit to letting them in?"

She claimed that no one quite saw who she was. It happened so fast. Rumors started flying about who did it.

I said, "It sounds like we have another mystery on our hands."

"Well, no one thinks letting in the dogs was intentional. They just ran in, in a pack."

"Who do you suspect opened the door?" I asked.

"I tried to figure it out, but no one on our floor quite fit the bill."

I asked her if the administration wanted to know who did it. She said that they didn't care much since the damage was done. I wanted to know that when the dogs ran in, where they went first.

She answered, "I think they made a beeline for Fanny's favorite dog Lily."

"What did Fanny do?"

"She beat them off with her cane, but it was too late. Lily was injured."

I brought up what she said before, that she was Fanny's rival. Did she want Muffin after she lost Lily?

"Fanny said she didn't want Muffin. But she didn't like me having a dog when she didn't. At the home, dogs were shared. I think she didn't want me to take Muffin as my own."

"Couldn't she get another dog?"

At this point she really opened up. "Can you replace a child? That's why I want to know what happened to poor Muffin. She's an angel now."

I never thought about little dogs becoming angels. At that moment I could see them. Little white bushy dogs in puppy cuts with little wings flying around, with their little white furry wings. Maybe that's what the chubbiness is all about. Those little cherub angels are always chubby, wearing a banner or something. Maybe the chubby dogs wore banners too.

While I was daydreaming about little angel dogs, Arbuckle went into the kitchen and came out with another sealed envelope. She said, "Here is a down payment on your bill."

21

THE MEAN BLUES

When I got outside, I opened her sealed envelope, Damn, another $10! I've got to be rougher with her. She's working me like warm putty. Maybe she doesn't have much money. Why in the world would she hire a private detective if she couldn't pay for it? Ever since I met her, I had to question her hard in order to get information about the case. Most of the time we just talked about my weight and how sickly I looked. Maybe she was trying to pay me with advice. Advice is very low calorie. And it's cheap. That wasn't going to put flesh on my bones. I stopped at The Sugar Shack for a bag of caramel corn.

My next problem was to get ready for Julie. I was walking past the Silver Wok when I saw pictures of their dishes in the window. I stopped in and asked for a copy of the menu. When I got home, I picked out a dish and cut out the picture to take over to Julie's. That should get me off the hook for tonight. After my morsel with her, I could raid her snack food. She can't complain if I eat more. Right? That's the whole idea.

On my way to Julie's I tried to figure out how Fanny could have corralled Muffin to jump in front of the lawnmower. The dog knew her and wouldn't be frightened. If she'd tried to frighten Muffin, the dog wouldn't have gone very far. The dog would've thought she was playing.

Fanny's so slow that even if she had a meat cleaver, she couldn't have gotten in a good swipe. What a picture, Blockman trying to take whacks at the little dog. I put it out of my mind. And if she was caught swinging at the little dog, she'd be sent back to Elysian Fields and put in a padded room.

I was carrying the picture of the Chinese dish when Lou and Pete spotted me. Those pests couldn't leave me alone. I was working on a case. They wish they had one.

I started in, "Why don't you guys go the dispatcher's office? Maybe somebody there'll want to talk to you."

Pete said coyly, "Aw Jack don't be sore. We see that you spend most of your day walking to Julie's. We're just making sure that no one accosts you."

"Why do you think anyone would attack me? Yeah, I'm a regular crime magnet."

Lou said, "Yeah crime follows you around. But shamus, you look so weak. It makes you a target. All we have to do is follow you and pick up the criminals as they are about to jump you. Make sure you eat something or you won't be strong enough to walk home."

There was a time when private detectives could work with police. At least in Hollywood movies, that's the way it was. These guys just spend taxpayer money riding around all day. Then a coffee break, then some donuts, then a few chilidogs, then more coffee, then free sweets from The Sugar Shack. No wonder those guys are misshapen. When they put their pants on, they hold the big gut up in the air with both hands while their wives tighten their belts underneath it. They then rest the size XXXL on top of the belt. Ready for work.

Julie wasn't very happy. I think the mean blues were starting. That's what happens when she's hungry. We didn't weigh in. It was only yesterday that we weighed in. She right away turned to my end of the bargain.

"What have you been eating today? You don't think that I'm going to suffer here starving while you pick your way through vending machine food?"

I said somewhat defensively that I had a substantial dinner. I knew it was a lie. But did you want her to eat my head off? We don't have to have a pitched battle tonight. It's too early in the diet. Tell her some soothing things and enjoy the evening.

Then she said, "Before we sit down to dinner, show me the picture of what you had for dinner?"

I whipped out the picture of my Chinese dish.

"That doesn't count. You could've gotten that picture anywhere. I expect you to bring a photo of the dish."

I explained to her that I'd need a Polaroid camera to get a quick picture. I had to be at her place only an hour later.

"You should get one. How am I to believe you? Give me that picture." She grabbed it from my hand. "If you ate this dish, you would know what was on the plate. What vegetables were on the plate?"

I didn't count on being quizzed. I knew it was a beef dish.

"How am I supposed to know. You know I don't like vegetables. So, I throw them away."

"Then you didn't eat this dish."

"I didn't eat the whole thing."

That's how it went. Afterwards, we went over to the sacrificial table with the tablecloth and lit candle in the middle. I put the morsel in my mouth, didn't chew, and it was gone. Dinner's now over fast. No pleasant conversation. No, "How was your day honey?"

I said, "Since you want me to eat more, I'll go to the pantry to get in a few snacks to add calories to my big meal."

"You're cruel. I don't want you chomping on chips or pork rinds while I'm starving over here."

I looked in the pantry.

"What did you do?"

"I gave all of my snacks to my neighbor."

"How're you going to fatten me up if you don't have food around?"

“Your food is your problem. I’m keeping my end of the bargain.”

See what I mean by “the mean blues.” We didn’t have a bargain. She manipulated me into this diet thing. As I expected, we’d ride the diet ball bearing around and around the track for the next few weeks.

I did tell Julie about my suspecting Fanny but had no idea how she could’ve pulled it off. Julie right away said that if she were this immobile heavy-set woman, she’d poison the dog. When she said it, it made sense. A little rat poison and the dog would be gone. I had that angle to work on.

22

SHORTAGE OF SYRUP

I limped home on fumes. People wanted me to gain weight and kept nagging me about eating. Then they didn't come through with food. Not that I'd have eaten it. They'd at least been in my corner. Instead, I was supposed to bankroll this lavish diet to please them. I don't mind criticism, but they won't let it rest. Every time they saw me, they started in again. What bothered me was that they're all overweight. Those boys in blue had their front seats in the cruiser set all the way back. Otherwise, their bellies would be wedged against the steering wheel so they wouldn't be able to turn. At least I wasn't overweight.

Outside my front door was a bag of stale donuts. I knew it was a bag of stale donuts because someone had written on the bag in big magic marker "STALE DONUTS." Of course, they didn't sign their name. That's the kind of respect I get. They were thinking of me and trying to get my goat. Recycle the donuts through old Jack rather than throw them out. I needed some sustenance. I didn't blink an eye. I wasn't proud. I especially liked the chocolate-topped ones with the jellies inside.

I got a can of pop out of the fridge and went to town on the donuts. Julie's comment about the dog being poisoned stuck in my head. Kill the dog, mutilate it, put the remains at the top of a tree. That didn't make sense. The dog could only be killed once. So why go through the bother? Kill the dog and leave. It makes you think of some twisted bastard who wasn't satisfied just killing the dog.

The poison idea was good because I had something I could investigate. It's the old story of the drunk under the streetlamp looking for his keys. "I lost them in the dark over there; I'm looking for them here because that's where the light is." I had no other pressing work. I had time to see where this case led. Tomorrow I'd go back to Elysian Fields and nose around. See if there was poison around. Fanny didn't strike me as particularly competent and mobile. If she did poison the dog, it couldn't have involved great effort on her part.

I was able to sleep in a couple of hours after dawn because I taped some newspaper over the tear in the shade. It looked awful, but it did the trick. I needed the sleep. I had trouble digesting those greasy donuts. No wonder they were stale. Whoever had them didn't want to finish the bag. I should've learned my lesson. You can't sleep on a heartburn special. Heartburn is the pits. It's worse than hunger. Greasy donuts conjure up all that acid. You just lay there and burn and think about when's it going to end.

On my way out I bumped into Stan who seemed in a hurry. I told him I just got paid and I'd like to take him to breakfast this morning. I asked him because I saw he was in a hurry and wouldn't take me up on it. My ten-dollar check wouldn't have covered both of us anyway. He said, "I can't make it Jack. I'm on my way to a job interview. Maybe we can get together another day?" "You got it Stan." You might suspect that I was setting him up for it being his turn to offer later in the week.

I headed down to the diner for my cup of black coffee and some pancakes with syrup. My favorite gal Mabel was behind the counter.

Mabel said, "Hey Jack, haven't seen you in a while."

"I haven't been hungry lately."

"You look like you should eat a horse."

"It's not on the menu."

"You should take better care of yourself."

I don't know why I immediately bring out the inner mother in people. If I followed all of their advice, I would be bigger than the boys in blue. No wonder they had flat feet. It's not from walking. They just stood up and pop when their arches.

"Working on any good cases lately?"

"Yeah, Mabel, I'm working on a big case involving the mysterious death of a little dog."

"Was a crime committed?"

"Destruction of property or cruelty to animals might be as far as it would go. My client wants to know how the death came about. The dog was mutilated and found at the top of a tree."

"Gruesome."

"Yeah, it kind of breaks your heart that somebody would do that to a little dog. When I solve the case, I'll come in to celebrate and tell you all about it."

"I'll get that horse and put it on a plate for you."

When Mabel brought the pancakes, I was ready for the bottle of syrup. I asked her for it. I always put about half a bottle on my pancakes. Mabel said, "We switched over to those little packets of syrup."

Then she reached in her apron and gave me two. Two? A man can't live on two. The pancakes will be doughy and dry. They'll make me gag.

"I like to drown the pancakes in syrup Mabel. Could I have a few more?"

"Sure Jack. Here are a couple more."

Breakfast turned out disappointing. I couldn't finish the pancakes. At least I had my cup of dark coffee. After a couple of cigarettes, the nicotine brought me to the point where the syrup would have. I'll have to hoard those little packets of syrup and bring my own next time. There'll be about forty empty wrappers next to my plate when I leave next time. I made a mental note of that.

23

RAT CONTROL

Elysian Fields was scenic as ever. The designers of these places always think that a dose of nature will cure people. When you're psychotic or suffering from a lot of chronic diseases, the last thing you care about is trees, ponds, and birds. I know from life experience. When I'm sick, I don't care about anything but the agony. Maybe the serene setting isn't for them but for the staff and visitors. Make the staff satisfied with their low wages. Make the visitors want to come back. Help sooth their guilt about their mother or father being in such a place. Or at least make them sign the checks when the bills come due.

Keep that picture of the groomed surroundings in mind. The peacefulness of it all. The lovely woodland setting. The rolling green grass. The ponds and water features. Now picture this. Imagine that you see a dirty rat running across the lawn. A big stealthy one, the size of a cat. A sewer rat with a greasy coat.

Did it spoil the picture? It wouldn't look right. Right? Your attitude about the place would change. Your focus would narrow. You'd just be worried about that rat.

I went to the maintenance building. That's where you would sometimes find maintenance people. They would hang around there a good part of the day. They would come in to check the big board that told them what to do next. The first guy I ran into said his name was Ozzie and he wanted to help me.

I said, "My name is Jack Smith, and I'm writing a report on how excellent a job institutions do in controlling for rats and insects."

"You a newspaper reporter?"

"I'm hired by the county to write the story. The idea is to give the public a good sense for how well managed Elysian Fields is."

I figured this would make Ozzie open up and brag about all they did to keep pests under control. I was right. He didn't want to stop talking. Some of it, though, was whistle blower stuff, but he didn't realize it. "What arsenal of poisons do you use for rats?" He took me over to a rack and showed me several cans. Yep. There was enough poison there to kill every living thing at Elysian Fields.

I asked him if the bait traps were set in the manor house—insurance that vermin would be killed. After all, they're usually nocturnal. He said that they had traps all over the place, but they try to hide them. That's so residents and visitors don't get the impression that the place is infested. I thanked him for his help and that I could now write a very good report.

What I found out showed that Fanny had the means for poisoning darling Muffin. Did she have the gumption? That's another question. She must've had a lot of help doing it. It's difficult to come up with a group of seniors, who can hardly move around, joining some conspiracy to off the little dog. I was thinking about all of this on my way back to the city. I decided that my next stop would be the crime lab.

24

NARCISSA

I had a friend at the crime lab. I had to sneak into the lab because I wasn't supposed to be in there. Lou and Pete would find some way to make my life miserable over it. I made my way into the back of the building. There I spied my buddy.

"Hey Narcissa, are you busy?"

"Hey Jack-o-Lantern. Going to bring me some light?" She then started with this nervous giggle of hers—Te, he, he, he, Te, he, he, he. Narcissa was a real high-flyer. In the story so far, you probably think I'm a weirdo. No. Narcissa's the weirdo. She's supposed to be a scientist and careful worker. Just watch her. She's constantly distracted. She's so distracted that she distracts herself from her distractions. She never stops moving. She darts around like she never wants to focus on anything. I don't think she ever sleeps. Sort of like a shark.

Like me, she's skinny as a rail but much taller. I guess you have to be a weirdo to work in that lab. When I asked her whether she was busy, of course she was busy being distracted. I just distracted her a little more. She then said, "Got any interesting corpses to work on?"

"Naw, I left all of the interesting ones in the car. People call me a walking corpse."

"I don't want to work on you, especially while you're moving. Te, he, he, he, Te, he, he, he."

"I always try to be quick. They say life belongs to the quick."

That's got to be true. That's what life is. A moving corpse isn't a corpse. Oh, maybe on Halloween it can move. That's when it's haunted. The rest of the year it stays put. Anyway, I cut to the chase and asked her about poisons. She said and I quote, "I like poisons. They give me more to study."

She's a really weird gal. I asked what kind of poison is used to kill rats.

"Metal phosphides work very well."

"Now suppose that a little dog eats some of it, how long before the dog dies?"

"Depends upon dosage."

"Would a rat dose do it?"

"I think so, usually, Te, he, he, he, Te, he, he, he."

There's nothing funny about what I just said. I can crack that girl up all day. Well not really. I'll bet she laughs like that to herself when I'm not there.

"A little dog was killed with poison?"

"That's the case I'm working on. I don't know if it was poison but it kind of looks like it. Some creep then mutilated the dog and threw it up in a tree."

"Now there's a distorted bastard, Te, he, he, he,Te, he, he, he."

"The remains of the dog are in the Heaven's Rest pet cemetery, and I was wondering if I brought you a sample, if you would test for poison."

"That's an awful lot of trouble. Why is this cutie pie worth it?"

I told her it's a long story. A nice old lady who is a bit disturbed treated the dog like it was her only friend in the world.

"You want to make her feel better by proving it was poisoned? That should make her jolly. Te, he, he, he, Te, he, he, he."

No wonder Narcissa was hidden back there in that lab. How could she pass a serious job interview while laughing her way through it? Especially when they get to the off-color parts of the interview.

"Will you test a dog specimen?"

"Only if you promise me the next real corpse you work on."

"Deal."

Narcissa puts together distracted bits and pieces of her day and gets the job done. She writes these sociopathic evidence reports. You wonder what uptight scientist wrote them. No "Te, he, he, he, Te, he, he, he" jokes in them. Of course, right now I don't need a report. I might need one later on. If the two screws saw me there, they would make her bill me. Or they would try to revoke my license. Or they would kick me out. Lou and Pete were real pals.

25

GREAT GREEK COMBINATION PLATE

The day was wearing thin, so I had to make some effort getting ready for Julie tonight. I borrowed a Polaroid camera from Narcissa, so I could take a picture of some food. I was walking past a Greek restaurant and there was Birdman Fritz eating a great Greek combination plate. I hurried in.

"How you doin' Birdman?"

"Just fine Jack-man. Want to join me?"

"Sounds good."

I asked him if I could take a photo of his combination plate.

"That's strange. Why don't you order your own?"

"It's a long story. It has to do with Julie being on a diet and wanting me to gain weight."

"That makes your wanting the picture clear as mud. Get on with the picture so I can get back to eating."

I took my picture. I thought boy will Julie be surprised. I knew she didn't think I'd do it. The downside was it gave her another excuse to badmouth me. You know, when she's suffering with her diet and thinks about my combination plate. I ordered up a little wine and a baklava.

"How's the dog case coming? The cops seem to have your number."

I told him that they're always harassing me. It breaks up

their day. "The bums blew the whistle on me to my client and she tore into me for two hours. That lady was inconsolable. Finally, I changed the subject to food. She enjoys needling me about my diet."

"Too bad Jack-man. Are you any closer to solving who killed the dog?"

"I was just talking to Narcissa at the crime lab and she can prove whether the dog was poisoned."

"Why would you think the dog was poisoned?"

"This other old lady was a rival of my client and I think she could've poisoned the dog."

"What about the dog being mutilated and ending up in the tree?"

I told him that Narcissa can prove once and for all if the dog was poisoned. We can try to answer the other questions later.

"Suppose the dog was poisoned. You don't know that the old lady did it."

I said, "Well we're proving there is a poisoner. The poisoner poisons the dog. Muffin was poisoned. So, the lady had to poison the dog."

"Sounds like you are going to blame the lady if the dog was poisoned? You have to show she was a poisoner."

I didn't quite get his point, so I said that once we know how the dog died, I can collect my check and move on.

We arranged to meet later at the gate of Heaven's Rest. Fritz agreed to help me dig up the dog and take a sample. I had my food picture. It was time to move on to Julie's. When she's on a diet, you don't know what you're going to walk into. I was dreading the evening. I knew that it would be emotionally all over the place. Somehow I was always on the receiving end of Julie's grand diet plans. She'll be mean, but I hope she lost some weight. That might make her verbal jabs worth it.

26

LIVE FOR TODAY

As I walked into Julie's, she was beaming.

"I was talking to Fran, and she saw you in that Greek restaurant eating dinner."

That was good news.

"I got together with my buddy Fritz to compare notes and plot strategy for our next move on the dog caper."

"Did you take a photo of your meal?"

"I borrowed a Polaroid camera from Narcissa at the crime lab. Here's my plate."

"I'm really surprised. I've been working hard at my diet. I even got more exercise than usual. Tomorrow we'll weigh in and see some results."

Oh my god. She expected to see results after only a couple of days. What was I to do? This was going to take some figuring out.

"Do you feel a little lighter?"

And she turned on a dime.

"I always feel light. I'm light on my feet. I never said that I felt heavy."

I tried to recoup my good attitude and said that I knew she never said such a thing. I said that I should've put it more accurately. "Do you feel better?"

"I'm feeling optimistic. I'm going to be a new me. And I'm

going to see a new you shape up before my eyes."

I said, "That's a positive scene. Our couple-dom is forming right in front of you."

With every word, her high-flying expectations were taking over. The whole thing'll come crashing down when she doesn't lose weight and I don't gain any. I suppose we should live for today. If that doesn't work, live for the moment. If that doesn't work, live for the minute. You know what I mean. Push the damn looming horror of it all to the background. Cherry pick the few happy moments. I've been trying to do that with Julie ever since I met her. But she's been trying to make herself better in her own eyes and a step on that path is to make me more suitable.

I noticed that Julie was studying me more than usual. She was staring at me. Being self-conscious crept over me. Maybe I should've pinched my cheeks to give them a rosy color. I could've put cotton balls in my mouth to reduce the sunken look. I could've worn some extra shirts to make it look like I had a build. Anyway, this was the sort of thing that flashed through my mind. I was always trying to defend my way of life.

The candle was lit on the dining room table again. The usual two big plates and a little morsel lost in the center of each. I don't get it as to why looking at that tiny bit of food on that barren desert of a plate helped anything. It could only remind Julie how hungry she was and it made me just want to get it over with. I suppose for Julie it represented her steely will to stick to the diet. We sat down. One gulp and it was over.

My dog used to eat like that. You filled up this big bowl. He'd run in and GULP it was all gone. He then looked around and looked around like, "Where's my dinner? I'm ready. I'm ready." They have short memories those dogs. My memory of my morsel was like that. Don't quiz me about what morsel I ate. "Where's my dinner, where's my dinner?" Forget about dinner? I don't remember a dinner. Blow out the candle and let's move on.

I told Julie about Narcissa and how she thought that poor little Muffin was rat-poisoned. How Fritz and I were about to go grave robbing in the dead of night. She thought we were crazy. Why not talk to Arbuckle and get a sample the legal way? Julie always made sense when I didn't want her to.

"Aw, why go through all of that rig-a-ma-roll? Arbuckle would be beside herself again and I'd be the whipping-boy for hours. Why not just sneak in and get it over with. Nothing is harmed in the process."

Julie reminded me that the boys in blue were watching me. That was true. The only thing they do well is follow me around and irritate me. She then said I've not shown any wrong-doing in the dog's death but I've broken some laws myself.

She was right. I created a deficit in the crime leger. I was the one committing crimes. Small ones. The kind that no one should pay any attention to. The boys in blue were just picky. Picky just when it came to me.

"Julie, I was hired to get to the bottom of it. You have to crush apples to make cider."

I don't know if that made any sense, probably not, but she didn't have a comeback.

I decided to head back to the castle and get ready for the cemetery work. When I got back home, there was a note on my door, "STAY AWAY FROM THE DOG." That was odd. Who had a stake in all of this besides Arbuckle, Fanny, and me? I assumed the dog was Muffin but I couldn't be sure. Arbuckle would have a heck of a time climbing my stairs. Fanny even more so. Maybe I flushed out another player. Somebody who didn't want the truth revealed. This was just like in a murder mystery. All of a sudden, I felt professional.

27

THE CHINESE CARTON

The next night I met up with Fritz. It had already started raining. I knew that the boys in blue would be nowhere near here. They don't like rain. They would be hiding out, keeping warm and dry, in some coffee shop where they could hit the owner up for free coffee. No one would rob the coffee shop while the boys in blue were at the counter. The free stuff is just a courtesy for their deterrent effect. So, there we were, Fritz with a pail and steak knife and me with the shovel and flashlight.

I told Fritz about the note. He thought that someone was pulling my leg. Having a belly laugh about it. Tweaking my nose about the magnitude of the case. I began to see it his way. No one I talked to seemed to think much about the dog's death except Arbuckle and me. And she was paying me. The joke's on me, Ha Ha. Fritz said he would be surprised if the note indicated a real threat. Ok, maybe I was looking at the note through rose-colored glasses.

The rain kept pelting down. It felt like the scene of a real mystery— the dark night, the rain, the cemetery, digging up a grave. We got to Muffin's plot. It was the same as when we left it. We dug up the vault, opened the casket, and using the steak knife in as artful a way as we could, cut out a chunk of Muffin. We put the grave back as before. I put the sample into a little baggie and into the pail. That was easy. We seemed good at it. I was glad that Fritz decided to join me. He said that he was interested in the eagle and he wanted to see if there was any connection to the dog. He was really interested in the fate of that eagle.

I said, "Well, we'll compare notes after the tests are done."

I went back to my place. I saw a Chinese take-out carton at the back of the fridge. I tried to hold my nose when opening it and tried not to look. Pee-Yuu. I emptied out this awful looking congealed and hairy-looking mess. I washed the carton. I put the Muffin sample into the carton, and labeled it "dog specimen." I put the specimen in the fridge and got ready for bed. Tomorrow I'd get some answers.

Then god knows what time it was in the middle of the night, there was this terrible BAM, BAM, BAM at my door. I looked through the peephole and there were Lou and Pete looking none too happy. I said through the door,

"Go away, do you want to wake up the whole building?"

"We have a search warrant. Open up."

I opened the door. As they barged in, Lou held the warrant up close to my face so I couldn't read it.

"Where were you tonight?"

"Right here sleeping as I always do."

"A surveillance camera was installed at the gate to the pet cemetery and we caught a glimpse of you guys going in," Lou said.

"We were just cutting through the cemetery. We had other business."

"What business? You know the cemetery closes at 11 PM and you were there at quarter after."

"Sorry I wasn't paying attention to the time officer Lou." Then Pete says, "I'll look in the fridge Lou." He sauntered over to fridge and opened the door. There was my carton.

"Hey Lou, there's dog in this carton."

I said, "That's why it's labeled 'dog specimen'."

He peeked into the carton. "Holy cow Lou, there is dog in there."

Pete and Lou hovered over the carton looking in. Some of the odor of the dead Chinese dinner surrounded the carton along with the putrid smell of decaying dog.

"Holy shit, this is awful," Pete said. "I know you eat funny Jack. You even look like the kind of guy that eats dog. But rotten dog?"

"That's what he was doing in the cemetery. He was digging up his next meal," said Lou. "Holy shit. That's why we caught him there three times. This guy's a real pervert."

I said, "Leave my specimen alone. I'm going to have it tested tomorrow."

"I want to know if it came from the Muffin dog? How could you eat the Muffin dog?" asked Lou.

"Of course not, I'm working on another case and the owner gave me this sample."

"You've got a corner on dead dog investigations. We'll check on that."

Pete said, "Yeah, he's a specialist."

I was so groggy. As they spoke, I began to realize that they couldn't get a warrant. No felony was on the table. At worst, they had me for cutting through the cemetery a little after it closed.

"Let me see that warrant again. Hey this isn't a warrant, it's just some letter. Time to leave guys and go to the gym to work off those bay windows."

Lou said, "You're up to no good shamus. You're into something weird and we're going to catch you."

"There's no crime in being weird."

He went on, "We're going to make sure it makes you unpopular. Get some sleep Jack. We'll see you tomorrow."

Of course I couldn't sleep. They'd check out my story. I didn't get it as to why they would. Oh sure, I know. They'd nothing better to do, and they didn't like me.

28

BOTULISM

I rolled in bed with my head going around. I was planning the day. I got up early, grabbed the dog specimen, and headed out. I didn't have time to tap Stan for breakfast, so I decided to give him a break. One way to get a quick continental breakfast is to cruise through the Hilton at the right moment. Out in the lobby by the meeting rooms, they put out a spread for conventioneers. After grazing it, they all go into meetings at usually seven thirty. The trays of pastries have a few stray items that no one wanted.

I was right on time. The lobby by the meeting rooms was almost empty. A few people were rushing here and there filling coffee cups to take into meetings. There was my target. Three Danishes were left. Yew! One of them had a bite taken out of it. Criminy! Who would take a bite out of it and then put it back? No wonder the other two right next to it were left. I grabbed the other two, moved on to filling a coffee cup, and headed for the exit.

I knew that Narcissa got to the lab early. She probably went through the door six times before sitting by the lab bench. She was so distracted. I guess she follows her head. What's in her head is so chopped up that she keeps changing course. Her behavior seems so random. She's like that Pimpernel guy; he's here, he's there, he's everywhere.

"Do you have something good for me Jack?"

I held up the carton and she laughed in that ninny voice of hers. I told her that the sample was well on its way returning to nature. She laughed again, "Te, he, he, he; Te, he, he, he." When I'm around that gal, I feel like I'm a standup comic. She should do laugh tracks for sit-coms. I asked if the state of the sample made a difference for the tests. She said no. Rat poison would still show up. I asked if I could wait until she finished the tests.

"Sure Jack. Pull up a stool. This is a really crude cut you made Jack."

"I did it with a steak knife."

"Yep, this dog has seen better days. No, this dog has seen better nights. Last night the surgery was botched."

We made light conversation while she took samples and ran various tests. I wanted to sit it out in the lab because I didn't want the boys in blue to find me. They'd never think of looking for me in the lab. I should go on the offensive and charge them with an unreasonable search. That'd take a lawyer, though, and cost me money I didn't have. What would I get out of it? No cash that's for sure. They knew that so they were free to harass me. The bums.

"Well, Jack my man, it wasn't rat poison."

I said, "Oh crap."

"It was botulism."

"Botulism? You mean that the dog ate some spoiled canned goods?"

"Very funny, Te, he, he, he. Te, he, he, he. Even scavengers can run into a foul piece of meat."

With that Narcissa began moving through the room this way and that. I tried to act as if everything was normal.

I said, "The little dog was no scavenger. Where would she get the botulism?"

"I don't know. You are the detective. Te, he, he, he. Te, he, he, he."

"Could she have run into the park and found a dead squirrel, chomped on it, got botulism and died on the spot?"

"Not likely. It takes a lot for botulism to develop in the wild, but it does happen."

"Where did it come from then?"

"If I had to lay odds, I would say it was in tainted dog food."

"So, the dog ate tainted dog food, ran into the park, and died on the spot?"

"That's one way it could've gone."

"My client could've, unknowingly, fed the dog the poison. Then there'd be no foul play?"

"That's one explanation."

"How else could it go?"

"The dog could have run into the park, and then, some shadowy figure fed the dog the poisoned food."

I said beaming, "Narcissa, you're a princess. I don't know what happened to the dog, but you showed that rat poison didn't kill him. I need to move in another direction."

She replied, "You may not know what you're doing Jack, but you bring me interesting problems to work on."

"That won't cost you Narcissa. I won't send you a bill." That woman was really solid. I couldn't ask more of a friend.

29

THE BEAN COUNTER AND THE BAD BAG

I mumbled out loud that Arbuckle seemed to live for the dog. She wouldn't have given her nasty dog food. Or maybe she had a dark side. It seemed more likely that Fanny was involved. Suppose Fanny had this nasty dog food left over from Lily. She knew the food was bad. She wanted to make Muffin sick. She stalked the dog to make it sick. It would come back into Arbuckle's apartment and mess up the rug. You know, barf, and then an exploding dust cloud would rise from the rug.

In that case, she wouldn't think she was going to kill Muffin, just sicken her a little. I liked that story so I decided to return to Elysian Fields and nose around. Every time I went there, I was struck with how beautiful the grounds were. I could camp out there. I happened to arrive around lunchtime when they have these little goodies. Finger food of one sort or another was set out on trays and residents, staff, and guests grazed a little. I found a few egg salad sandwiches but made a beeline for the table with the little pieces of chocolate cake. It took quite a few pieces to fill the void.

Of course, you can't just walk in and raid the food. You strike up polite conversations. I said I was there to see Miss Blockman, what a fine lady. Most everyone was glad to see an outsider. Seeing the same, mostly sad faces, wears thin. Staff try to preserve an air of normal society. Make it seem like this is the outside world, the classy outside world, and not an institution.

Except there was this hornet of an administrator. She was buzzing around the room. I kept my eye on her. She struck me as a bean counter. It was like she was calculating the cost of everything. When she saw me go after my fourth sliver of chocolate cake, she landed next to me and said,

"Have quite a sweet tooth over there?"

"Yeah, cake agrees with me."

"Don't you think you should leave some for the residents?"

"No one seemed to be interested in it but me."

"They are still eating their lunch. They aren't ready for dessert yet."

"Thanks for tipping me off."

The creep. She just didn't like seeing me enjoy the cake. The residents don't seem to enjoy anything. That's the way she liked it.

The hubbub of the luncheon continued. It was a slow and quiet hubbub. I slowly snuck out to walk around the building. I thought that dog food would go bad if it got wet. Suppose somebody kept a bag of food outside. If it were there long enough, it would mold. Sure enough, when I got to the West side of the building, there was a bag of dog food. When I looked in, it was all meshed together with green mold growing all over it. It looked just like the stuff that a dog barfs up when sick. I took a small sample of it. Narcissa might be able to give me an opinion.

I then went to Blockman's place to say hello.

"Fine day Miss Blockman. No rain expected."

And then she started up talking slowly,

"I swear I won't see you the next time you come in. Are you on a starvation diet? Are you in some movie about a disappearing man?"

"I'm doing the best I can. I'm so busy that I have little time to eat. If I disappeared, I would have a real case to solve— how I ended up disappearing." What a greeting. Disappearing man. She saw me, didn't she?

I moved on. I said I enjoyed our chat the other day. I was in the area and decided to stop by. Meanwhile, I inched over to her sliding glass doors and looked out. It wasn't where I found the bad dog food. I asked her that when Lily died, was there leftover dog food. She told me that she gave it to another resident who had dogs. The bad dog food I saw outside the other unit could have been hers.

I asked for her thoughts on the death of Muffin. The story was all over the news. Her recollection was that the dog had a good heart. She didn't understand why anyone would mutilate the poor animal and put it up in a tree. I told her that I was spending some time trying to figure that out. She asked if I could explain it. I told her that, as of right now, it beats me. She said that she was glad that someone was looking into it and that, that sort of thing shouldn't be allowed to happen. I told her I'd keep her in the loop.

30

THE DOG FOOD

I'd been steering clear of the phone all day. I assumed that the boys in blue had contacted Arbuckle about the dog chunk in my refrigerator. I figured that if she was calling in hysterics to dress me down, I would let some time pass. To let the dust settle so to speak. I also wanted to sneak around so the boys in blue wouldn't find me. I didn't need those numbskulls making up stuff and trying to make me feel low.

I headed back to the police lab where they wouldn't find me. Those guys probably never set foot in the lab. They've never investigated a case that required lab work. All they do is get fat on the public's dime. Narcissa was ricocheting around the lab as usual. She had so much stuff in there. You wouldn't think the city needed a major crime lab. Whatever she did all day, it was hard to put together until you asked her to write a report. The report would be spectacular. You would think that a Princeton scholar had written it.

"Back so soon Jack-man? You must have some more work for me. Right?"

"I can't stay away Narcissa. I need answers. What do you do all day in here?"

"I invent and run tests on all sort of things. You'd be surprised what I learn. If all I had to work on were cases, I would have too much focus. I have to stay nimble. It's all in how you inquire. You bring me a problem and I'll have a strategy for solving it."

"You're my woman Narcissa. Here's some bad dog food I found at Elysian Fields."

"I didn't know they had dog food there."

"Well, a suspect lives there. I found the decayed food outside on a patio some doors down."

"Decayed huh. Te, he, he, he. Te, he, he, he."

She knew I was looking for botulism, the sort that killed Muffin. It didn't take her long until she said,

"You get the grand prize. Same botulism."

"Amazing, I must be on to something."

"As a smart ten-year-old once said, 'could be' to everything. Te, he, he, he. Te, he, he, he."

"What do you mean? The bad food is conclusive proof."

"Could be. Botulism infected dog food could be all over the city."

"But you said it was exactly the same strain."

"Sure, but for all we know, it might be a common strain. Te, he, he, he. Te, he, he, he."

Why did she have to tell me that? She could've left me to enjoy the moment for a while. Kill joy. After all this work we end up with the dog being killed by botulism in dog food. Some of that kind of food was at Elysian Fields.

I didn't let Narcissa get me down. There was still an evidence trail to follow. I decided to return home to face the music. I thought that I wouldn't play back my answering machine. My message box was full. And guess who filled it? Not Publishers Clearing House hounding me all day about having won a couple hundred thousand dollars.

Rather than let her catch up to me, better to go on the offensive. I'll call her. Maybe I can catch her off guard so that it will take a while for the big emotions, tears, and shouting to begin. I might even get a word in every now and then.

"Hello, Miss Arbuckle, this is Jack the shamus."

I was surprised that the tearful part of the day was over. She was mean from the start.

"You ghoul, eating dead animals for dinner. You scavenger. I don't care if you prey on the destroyed carcasses behind the animal shelter. How did my Muffin taste? Putting her in a Chinese carryout carton. Shame on you. Shame on you." The boys in blue had worked their magic. The fabricators. The ne'er-do-wells.

"They found a lab specimen in the carton. It wasn't Muffin." I had lied to Lou and Pete about this, so I had to keep the lie going. I then added, "I've never eaten dogs or any other pets." Now that's true.

"Your refrigerator had all of this decayed food pushed into the back. The carton with my Muffin in it was the only thing right up front. Were you saving it for a snack?"

"I had this other dog sample to take to a lab. You know you aren't my only case." She hesitated.

"What about the other dog?"

"Another dog died in the park under mysterious circumstances just like Muffin. I'm testing that dog at the police lab to see if it helps me with figuring out what happened to Muffin."

Her tone improved when I mentioned the police lab.

"Why should I have anything to do with you, you desecrator?"

"I should have some answers when the lab report comes back."

"Why were you and the other grave robber sneaking around the cemetery again?"

"My friend is a specialist that I call on in certain cases. I'll explain it all when I get some results."

At this point I wish I'd listened to Julie. I should've explained the tests for poison, gotten permission to exhume the corpse. Taken a sample for the lab. You know, acted professionally. Instead it seemed more exciting to prowl the graveyard with a shovel.

If the boys in blue weren't so nasty, none of this blowback

would have happened. Those guys are tattlers. Snitches. I wasn't very smart. I should've created a diversionary tactic. Like some great donut giveaway across town. Anyway, it was too late now. Miss Arbuckle seemed conflicted. What I cared about was whether I had finessed the situation to the point where I was going to get paid. I know. I'm not good at finesse.

31

MY FOOD STASH

I was so preoccupied on my way to Julie's that I only remembered at the last minute, as I was going into her building, that I was naked. I had no picture. I backtracked to my car and pulled the Polaroid camera from my back seat and set out to find a restaurant. I'd also forgotten to eat, so it was going to be painful to see dishes of food. I had to take a picture of somebody's plate before they ate much of it. Sure they'd be upset if I dawdled and gawked. I had to rush in, attack, and quickly exit. Before they would've realized it, I'd taken a picture.

The Thai place, Mango Heaven, came up first. I cruised through the dining room. There were no full plates on tables. On to the Italian place, Pasta, Pasta, Pasta. A number of plates were heaped with pasta. I circled, readied the camera, and made a quick pass. I came around again and shot. "Hey, you! Whadda you doin?" With that, I bolted. When I was down the street, I saw that my picture caught only half of the plate, and it was blurry. Julie wouldn't buy it that I took an action shot of my plate. I could explain, "As my plate was heading toward the table, I jumped up. . . ."

Next came the expensive steak house Burlington's. I wasn't dressed for the place. There was a couple sitting at a window table. They'd just gotten big steak dinners. I cocked the camera, hovered over them outside the window, and took the shot through the window. The picture had a few reflections but the plate looked great. I knew I'd need to make up a story about it because I didn't have money and even if I did, I wouldn't eat there.

I was late for Julie's, famished, and had only my morsel dinner coming in the near term. When I walked in, I heard voices. Not heavenly voices. There were the boys in blue sitting at the table chatting with Julie.

"They couldn't find you Jack, so they stopped by, figuring that you'd be here for dinner."

Great. What did they have in front of them? Chips and pop. My nerves were lit like a Christmas tree. Apparently, that thief Julie stashed my food when this diet thing started. Now the robust boys in blue were eating my food.

"Are you guys always hungry?"

"It was getting near dinner time, and Julie was nice enough to tide us over."

My complexion normally was grey-white, but now I was beet red. Julie knew I was pissed. I felt like going around in circles on one leg. I felt like going outside and pulling the fire alarm to get them to leave.

"The officers said that you were digging up animal graves."

"No. I was just passing through the pet cemetery. They like to make stuff up. They like drama. They also like food."

"They said that you had a chunk of dog in your refrigerator and that it was decayed."

I said that I'd told her about one dog case. Well, there was another dog case and the client gave me a sample for testing. I reached over to the bowl of chips to take a few.

"Didn't you just have a big dinner?"

"I can't resist chips."

"What're you guys doing here anyway? Did you just stop over to eat my snacks?"

"We wanted to keep you up to date on things. We checked

out your story. We wanted to tell you that it seems legit. You looked suspicious carrying that equipment through the cemetery after hours. What you did might just be innocent," Lou said.

Those guys couldn't investigate their way out of a paper bag. They probably talked to Fritz, and he kept to the story line.

"What were you doing in the cemetery after hours with a shovel?" Pete asked.

"As I said, we were just passing through. My fashion accessories aren't the usual ones."

"Yeah, you complement your wardrobe with a shovel and bathroom scale. Har. Har." Lou joked.

"I picked up those fashion tips from the East Germans. Didn't it dawn on you guys if I needed anything from a grave, I'd ask permission. Get legal approval?"

At that point, Julie beamed. That was her point last night.

"Maybe, but why all the sneaking around in the dead of night?" Lou asked.

"You guys are too suspicious. You think you see crime everywhere. Lighten up. I'm a private investigator. I'm on your side."

"There's a tall tale. You're only on the side of getting paid. You work in that dark place between the law and crime." Lou said.

"I'm investigating the mysterious death of a poor little dog. You guys don't want to do it. Do you?"

Pete answered, "We can't see that a law was broken. No one asked us for help."

"See, it's just a mystery. I'll get to the bottom of it."

Lou and Pete needed a place to hang out so they bettered community relations at Julie's. I don't know why Julie humors them. Oh, I do know. She just tries to irritate me and gets her jollies that way. I was feeling light-headed. I told the boys that I was feeling sick. They'd better leave so Julie and I could get on with the evening.

Lou said, “We’re going to keep an eye on you Jack. Ha. Ha. You’re not going to slip one by us.”

Julie could tell that I was at wits end. She tried to smooth things over. She lit that damned candle again and I swallowed my morsel whole.

“What’s for dessert?” I tried to press her.

“Let’s weigh in so we can see our progress. I’ll give you a nice dessert if you gained as much as I lost.”

She mounted the scale. She was down a pound.

“That’s not bad for a few days Julie.”

I mounted the scale.

In a pained tone she said, “Oh no. You lost two pounds!”

I tried to explain to her that with all the stress of the diet, the cops persecuting me, and the difficult case, I was burning calories at record levels. Even big meals didn’t give me a chance to put pounds on. I had a high metabolism. She didn’t buy any of it.

“Where’s the picture of your meal tonight?”

I whipped out my polaroid— “a big steak dinner.”

“That’s impressive. Where’d you get the money for such an expensive meal?”

“I found a coupon for a free entre.”

“Why aren’t you wearing good clothes after coming from a fancy schmancy place like that?”

“I went home to change. That’s why I was late.”

“Why are those reflections in the picture?”

“I don’t know. I’m not good at polaroid pictures.”

Her suspicions kept mounting. But she’d quizzed me so much already that she didn’t have the anger to push on further.

32

PLOP GOES THE EAGLE

On my way home, I wondered about my next step. I was so tired. I just wanted to hit the sheets and worry about the case tomorrow. Julie forced on me the idea that I needed to do something about my weight. I was beginning to agree with her. I looked bad. I felt bad. What else was new? I could duck out on the diet by saying I needed medical help. She might even be sympathetic to that. I could make the appointment for off in the future. That way I'd get a break from being held under the diet microscope. At least I wouldn't be the sponge for Julie's anger about her own weight.

When I got to my door, there was another note to greet me. "LAY OFF THE DOG, OR ELSE." What in the world was that note doing on my door? It was strange. What did it mean, "Lay off the dog." The dog was dead. You couldn't lay on it. Probably some prankster. Not very funny. I thought my neighbors needed a better sense of humor. Use a funnier tone.

The apartment was pretty empty of food. I needed something to eat. I had a couple of candy bars in the freezer. That got me ready for bed. I unplugged the phone and slept like a bear in winter. Late in the morning, I awoke and quickly headed to the greasy spoon. I could clear my head with some cups of black coffee and cigarettes. Too bad cigarettes don't have calories. I'd be fat by now. I had a couple of prime glazed donuts.

"Hey Mabel. Ready to donate some stale baked goods to the homeless shelter?"

"Maybe later in the day Jack."

I helped out the homeless by delivering the stale baked goods. Along the way a couple of coconut donuts would disappear. A man needs fuel for the delivery.

I decided that I needed to wrap up the botulism angle. Fritz had an interest in the eagle, and he did want to know how the tests came out. I stopped by. Fritz was humming away on some opera chorus while watching the toucan.

"Birdman. The little dog died from botulism caused by bad dog food. The food had to be really bad to kill her. Whoever gave it to her knew that the food would make her sick."

"There's mal-intent. Who would want to off the dog that way? Not the owner?"

"Miss Arbuckle isn't on my list. Besides if I proved she did it, when I would say, 'You did it', I wouldn't get paid."

"What's your next step Jackyl?"

"I was hoping you'd have some ideas. You were interested in the eagle."

Fritz thought the eagle wouldn't touch bad dog food. He said the eagle might have eaten some of the dog and the poison got to him later.

I said, "That'd tie the eagle to the dog. The head of the dog was missing."

"Well suppose the eagle ate the head off the dog. The eagle flew home. He's sitting on his perch. An hour later, PLOP. Like a rock, right to the ground."

"The owner wouldn't know what to think."

"The sad owner takes an eagle sculpture from his yard and uses it at the pet cemetery."

I said that the owner would have no idea the little dog in the next grave was missing a head and that that's what killed his eagle. Fritz and I looked at each other having the same idea. We needed to test the eagle for botulism.

I said that we had to get a sample. Narcissa at the crime lab knew the exact strain of botulism that killed the dog. If it showed up in the eagle, that'd be like a fingerprint. Well not exactly a fingerprint. I wasn't trying to be exact.

I explained to Fritz that the cops were shadowing me. Getting caught one more time in the cemetery would cause legal problems. Besides, I pleaded innocent. I committed myself to go the right route and get an exhumation order. Julie was counting on me doing that too.

We couldn't go to the eagle's owner. The boys in blue probably tipped him off that Alfie's grave was disturbed. They most likely spilled the beans about it being us. We were caught on the security camera at the gate. The owner probably thought we're weirdos. We can't just show up to ask for a specimen. He won't trust us.

"I don't know Jack, maybe he would like to know how the dog died and if it was related to Alfie's death."

"What if he said no. What would we do then? And he might alert the cops to our paying him a visit."

Fritz said, "If the cops caught us under those circumstances, we'd be in for some penalties. We just want to know if the eagle died from the same poison."

Ok, then we needed another approach. We needed a plan.

Fritz thought about it. He said that we should be the good guys this time. We should prove to the cops that we're the good guys. We get somebody else to dig up the bird and take a sample. Once he's clear of the cemetery, we call Lou and Pete and tell them we saw lights in the cemetery. They'd better come quick. An hour later when they arrive, we all look around only to discover the disturbed eagle grave. We'd be the good guys looking out for the cemetery and we'd have our sample. Brilliant plan!

33

JOHNNY O

I met Fritz for lunch to plan our caper. We met at the museum snack bar. I had one of those big pretzels, a cotton candy, and some deep-fried onion rings. Fritz had his usual chilidog. We both tried to think of somebody we could trust. I hit on an old buddy that used the homeless shelter. Johnny O was Native American. He was quiet and tied into the here and now. He didn't brag and was slow to give up information. He also was an imposing figure. He was tall, big boned, and had long black flowing hair. He cut an impressive image. We brainstormed his cover story.

Why would he dig up the eagle? Well, he was passing the pet cemetery when he noticed the eagle sculpture. The golden eagle was a sacred bird in his religion. To perform various rites, he needed an eagle feather. So, he took one feather from the grave and said some Indian words to smooth his theft over with the great spirits. Of course, he would've also taken a small sample for our tests. Good plan.

Later in the day, Mabel gave me the bag of stale donuts. On my way to the shelter, I ate a couple of deep-fried ones with the colorful crinkles on top. I asked for Johnny at the shelter. They said he was in the park near the river. There he was, sitting by a tree.

"How's life Johnny O?"

"I'm stayin' alive."

"You've got the fresh air. Nature is all around you."

"Homelessness isn't all it's cracked up to be."

"I've got a job for you. The pay is pretty good."

"I don't want to do anything dishonest."

I explained the plan and how full proof it was. He looked the other way when I gave him the cover story.

"What's your cover story?" he asked.

"I don't need one."

"I like it more when your ass is hanging out there too."

"You won't need the cover story. But just in case you're caught, just use the cover story."

"You like the cover story. What about the cops? Will they like it?"

I said that it wouldn't be beyond the truth that the eagle feather meant something important to him. He agreed. I think he needed the work. We arrived at satisfactory pay.

The plan was that Johnny would climb the fence into the cemetery to avoid the surveillance camera at the entrance. He would look for the eagle, dig up Alfie, take a feather, a sample, and return the grave to normal. When he was done, he'd shine his flashlight toward the hill behind the cemetery. Two flashes meant that he was clear to exit and about to climb the fence. We'd pick up his signal. We'd call the cops. It'd be a win win.

Earlier that evening, Fritz and I would make ourselves noticed walking up and down in front of the police station. We'd ask about Lou and Pete. We'd try to find them and make sure they didn't lose us. I'd stay with the cops in view while Fritz made his way to the hill. He'd wait for the signal. He'd join me. We'd drive past the cemetery. I'd stop and signal to the boys, "Look, there're lights over there!" Lou and Pete would invade the cemetery with us close behind. They'd notice the eagle grave has been disturbed. They'd realize that it couldn't have been us. We tell them that we were not responsible for the strange goings-on in recent days. Beautiful!

34

THE GRAVE-ROBBING GANG

As dusk settled in, we met with Johnny Ojibwa. We gave him the flashlight, shovel, a watch, and small specimen kit. We pointed to where the eagle sculpture was. We figured that it'd take about half an hour for him to finish up. We said that at 10PM, we'd begin looking for his signal. Two flashes in a row mean that it's time for us to signal the boys in blue. By the time they entered the grounds, Johnny would've been long gone. I'd meet Johnny the next morning at the homeless shelter to collect the sample and pay him. The plan seemed ironclad.

As dusk settled in, Fritz and I began looking for Lou and Pete. We checked their usual haunts: the park where they sleep in their patrol car, the establishments where they get freebees, and the place where they park and pretend to monitor speeding. No sign of them. We went to the police station.

"Where are Lou and Pete?"

"We don't know. They didn't check in lately. I think they're on assignment."

That "on assignment" thing was the catch-all for "we don't know where the hell they are." We decided to cruise up and down the street where they kept catching us and harassing me. No sign of them.

We began to get the creeping hunch that something was up. This was peculiar because Lou and Pete were as predictable as day and night. They were lazy except when making my life miserable. Oh oh! Maybe they were trying to do just that. Suppose they were hanging around Julie's. That'd be ok. She seemed to like their company. Poor girl. Where else might they be? Fritz and I looked at each other. Oh no! They were probably staking out the cemetery!

It was approaching 10PM, so Fritz and I went to the hill to wait for Johnny's signal. There was the signal. Flash, flash. Then a longish pause. And then flash, flash, flash, flash—Johnny just kept flashing. Something had gone wrong. We sped to the fence where Johnny was supposed to climb over. There was Johnny caught on top of the fence unable to free himself. That big guy was just dangling there. He had panicked— "HELP, HELP!" Coming up fast on the cemetery side of the fence were the boys in blue. Crap.

All four of us tried to free Johnny but he was at the top of the fence and was just too damned heavy. And he kept wiggling. Finally, Lou called the rescue squad. They had the right ladders to climb up and get him down.

The cops told the fire chief, "This guy was trying to rob a grave. You can tell by the shovel and flashlight he was carrying. And these others were his accomplices. They're the wheel men driving the get-away car."

Pete did the honors. "You're all under arrest."

Talk about embarrassment. Even the media began to show up. We were having our moment of fame. TV, newspaper reporters, the whole celebrity treatment. They took photos of every possible awkward position. What a nightmare.

So, we went to the station to get booked. Lou and Pete were beaming. They'd cracked the pet cemetery grave-robbing ring. I told Johnny not to say a word. I didn't have to because he was silent to a fault. We were all standing by the desk sergeant. He asked us,

"What did you guys want to get from the cemetery? Are you stealing the jewelry that owners bury with their pets?"

I said, "Only the diamonds and rubies. We only go for the big stuff. No flea collars or chewed up leashes. Come on! Who'd bury anything valuable with a pet?"

I decided that we needed a lawyer. We got a public defender. Rachel Ashcroft, our lawyer, couldn't believe the circumstances. She had this too serious look on her face. She hadn't been able to put together what the whole thing was about. I told her that at best, they had Fritz and me on aiding and abetting in a misdemeanor. Johnny was another story. We were jailed and would see a judge in the morning.

I called Julie to fill her in. She was sympathetic but angry. A kind of angry-sympathetic. "How could you be so stupid." She wasn't asking a question. She also began to show suspicion that we were serial grave robbers. The "that we just couldn't help ourselves" sort of thing. That attitude flashed "addiction," "support group," "big-time counseling." I hoped that she didn't begin to believe the twisted stuff that Lou and Pete were throwing around. We all felt bad for Johnny O. He was shouldering the burden. He was the perp. As Lou said,

"He's the leader of the ring. The mastermind. The MISTER BIG that to this point eluded detection."

35

IT'S ALL ABOUT RELIGION

The next morning, we appeared in court. Julie attended. Rachel did the talking. She wasn't making very much sense, so the judge wanted to hear from us what we were doing around the cemetery. Since the plan was mine, I decided to own up and talk for the group.

"Your Honor, our friend Johnny Ojibwa is a religious person. In his religious rites, he uses feathers like those of the golden eagle. The spirit of the eagle is in those feathers."

The judge interrupted, "This whole thing is about religion?"

"Yes sir. Johnny learned that a golden eagle was buried in the pet cemetery."

"How did he learn that?"

"I told him. Johnny then wanted to get an eagle feather from the dead eagle. I said to him, not so fast, the pet cemetery is private property. We talked about it. In the end, I didn't think it would hurt to take one feather, so we planned for Johnny to get his feather."

"Did Mr. Ojibwa pay you to help him?"

"No, we're friends. You know, friends help friends." " W h y were you and Fritz Obermeyer under mysterious circumstances showing up again and again at the pet cemetery? I was told that it was always in the dead of night carrying a shovel."

"I'm working a case. I'm looking into the death of a little dog named Muffin. Muffin died under mysterious circumstances, and she's buried right next to the eagle."

When you're spinning a story, it's better to keep it close to the truth. All of that can be shown. Leave the judge to sort out what's false.

"So, you told Mr. Objibwa about the eagle?"

"Sure did."

"Did you encourage him to dig it up?"

"No, that plan evolved slowly."

The judge observed, "Wouldn't the owner of the eagle have consented to Johnny having a feather? He might even have some spare feathers from when the eagle was alive. Did you contact the owner?"

"No. Sorry judge. I've some experience with owners of dead pets. They're sensitive. They don't like having their memories disturbed. You know there's a lot of hub-bub with an exhumation."

"Johnny, did you want the feather for religious purposes?"

"Uh huh."

"It looks like intended trespassing and vandalism. All of you are in on it, so I see no reason to single out Johnny. I'm glad you were forthcoming Mr. de Loosher. Lucky for you, Mr. Ojibwa didn't make it over the fence. He wasn't quite trespassing. If he were caught disturbing a grave, all of you would be in considerable trouble."

I almost choked. I had that sinking feeling. He didn't make it over the fence? The judge thought Johnny didn't make it into the cemetery. All he had on us was Johnny with the shovel getting caught on the fence and us coming to his aid. The whole cover story I told was volunteered information. I admitted to a plan to commit a crime that was never committed. Stupid. Stupid. There was no need for the cover story.

"Officers, do you have anything to add?"

Lou chimed in, "There's more going on here than they're letting on. I looked in Jack de Loosher's refrigerator and he had a Chinese carton with decaying dog in it. I think those two, (He pointed to me and Fritz), are up to something diabolical. Like eating spoiled dog meat that they dig up in the pet cemetery."

Rachel then said, "There's no law against eating bad dog meat."

I then said, "Who's eating bad dog meat? Not me. I'd labeled the carton 'dog specimen' not 'dog appetizer'; I was going to have it analyzed the next day."

Lou said, "Why was it in his fridge, right up front? That's where you put things you're going to eat."

Pete said, "Look at de Loosher, at how sickly he looks. It's his diet. Eating dead pets would explain it."

Rachel said, "How do you know what someone who eats dead pets would look like?"

Pete replied, "He would have bad skin, that ashen color, like the walking dead. Just like Jack."

Rachel then said, "There is no evidence here for what someone would look like if they ate dead pets."

Fritz added, "Better to eat dead pets than live ones."

Lou replied, "See, they even talk about eating live animals. They're up to something diabolical. They might be devil worshipers."

I said, "Can't you tell that Fritz was being sarcastic."

Pete responded, "They're not taking these charges seriously."

Rachel said, "The judge brought up only two charges, both misdemeanors."

With that, the judge said, "The police have been watching you guys, and I don't care if it's religion or a perverse diet or both. I'll say that you guys leave a mighty suspicious impression. I'd watch it, and stay out of the way of the police."

With that the judge fined us $100 each as well as court costs. We had to do twenty hours of community service cleaning up the pet cemetery. When he said that Lou blurted out,

"With all due respect your honor, you shouldn't let those guys anywhere near a pet cemetery. They may be casing their next job. How're we to tell if they're doing good or desecrating the resting places of sweet animals like Muffin?"

"I'll instruct the proprietors on how to monitor them when doing community service. If they slip up, and go after buried pets, they'll call in police like you two fine officers." Lou said, "Thanks judge. But these guys work after dark. They'll see some big appetizing pet buried during the day, and then they'll return at night to cut out the delectable parts. Well, delectable to them. Not to me!"

Pete said, "That guy Jack is a regular cannibal."

I said back, "A cannibal eats human flesh, not dog meat." Pete said, "You know what I mean judge. That guy cannibalizes these pets. You can say that he needs the food. Look how unhealthy he is. He should have other ways to get food."

"If you catch de Loosher doing anything like that, I'll lock him up."

Pete said, "The prison food would be better for him— maybe beef or fish or something."

With that, our court appearance was over. I could've brought up the fake search warrant and how Lou and Pete were following me around harassing me. But I thought better to let sleeping dogs lie. Outside the courthouse Julie cut into me about how deeply embarrassed she was and that I needed to improve my diet so that I didn't look half dead all the time. Reporters were all over the place, cameras blazing, swarming us. We made a run for it.

In all of the mayhem, I managed to get a word to Johnny. Why did the judge think Johnny got caught on the fence going into the cemetery? I told Johnny that he probably thought Lou and Pete would've caught him if he were inside. After all, they were staking out the place. He didn't know how inept they were. I wondered if Johnny got the sample. He should have. His signal was at ten o'clock before his wild flashing began.

He did.

All of this needless drama wasn't for nothing. Johnny O resisted slipping the sample to me because that was his ticket to getting paid. I told him I had the money to pay him tomorrow. He passed the sample to me. Fritz and I were on to visiting Narcissa at the lab in the morning.

36

DYNGUS DAY

I drifted off to sleep and then this noise startled me awake. There was this terrible racket in the building. I checked the clock and it was around 2 AM. Some kind of party was going on. As I sat up, I heard an endless stream of people coming and going. You know when somebody's door keeps being slammed, again and again, and with all those loud echoes in the hall. The party-goers weren't mellow. They sounded edgy. The usual way to avoid trouble was to invite all of your neighbors to the party and no one would complain. I guess I was in jail when the invitation went out.

I jumped out of bed when someone started banging on my door. BAM BAM BAM. "Come on Jack, put your party hat on." Sleep was impossible. I looked around frantically for my party hat. Where had I put the darned thing? Just kidding. Who has a damned party hat anyway? I joined them and thought I might catch up on some food.

Oh my lord. It was a Dyngus Day party. Catholics get wasted before lent, stay gray and long-faced till Easter, and then comes rip-roaring Dyngus Day. That's when history says Polish virgins were on the hunt for husbands. There didn't seem to be any virgins there. No Polish ones for sure. Come to think of it, there could've been just a couple of virgin wannabes. By the time I arrived everyone was wasted and ready for something else. Once down in Key West, a club goer told me, "You dance and drink until two in the morning. By then everybody looks good and you pair off." I guess that's one way to handle it.

Tables were full of all sorts of Polish food that I don't eat. Kielbasa, stuffed cabbages, and perogies don't agree with me. Too much gas. But thinking ahead, as I usually do, I ran upstairs to get the Polaroid camera. I loaded up a plate and took a picture of it to impress Julie tomorrow at dinner. I then took an "after" shot of one of the dirty plates with all manner of remnants from someone's meal. It would look like I ate the miserable sausages.

Now the Polish pastries were famous so I gorged myself on donuts, cheesecake, and gingerbread. I loaded up a plate to take upstairs for the fridge. Foraging is an important skill. It requires knowing your surroundings. And timing is everything. You have to know just when availability is at its peak and then harvest enough but not too much. You don't want the food to go to waste. I know, you're thinking I'm just blowing smoke. What about the back of my fridge? I have to put on rubber gloves and dive into the back where all of those penicillin-encrusted goodies wait for me. I hope it's penicillin and not some long-lost plague like The Black Death. Fear of The Black Death. That's it. That's what makes it hard to get up a head of steam to go back there.

Since my neighbors were as loose-lipped as I would ever find them, I made small talk and bridged into the notes on my door. More than one of them, actually two of them, said that when the buzzer for the downstairs door went off, they peeped through the fisheyes in their doors to see who was coming. They said it was a dark figure— the sort that casts a lot of shadow. They couldn't make out who it was because he wore a broad-brimmed black hat and a black trench coat with the collar turned up. Now really? If somebody like that would've been walking down the street, he would've stood out. You might think he were going to a costume party or something.

That's not the way to do a disguise.

The guy in the coat walked up to my door. Whoever it was knew where I lived. He put the note on my door with scotch tape. I tried to pick up on whether what the neighbors were saying was tongue in cheek. It was hard to tell. They were pretty poker-faced about it. They said he walked like a he-man. Sauntering and all.

I wondered if my neighbors could know that I was working on a dog case. But word spreads fast in the building. I know I'm paranoid, but it seems that they enjoy talking about me. I was all the rage after the media took pictures of the boys, Fritz, and me trying to get Johnny O off the fence.

On a gut level, so much attention was a compliment. Things were going on in my life. Maybe not always things you wanted to write home about. Maybe not things that you wanted going on in your life. But things were going on. If they had things going on, they wouldn't be talking about me. Some of the things going on in my life might make them lose sleep. They wouldn't know what was coming next. I didn't either.

I asked how the mysterious spook got into the building. Ella, my neighbor across the hall, said it was easy. All they had to do was push all of the buzzers and someone would let them in. Just like in 1940's film noir. This seemed a bit off to me. If someone went to the lengths of wearing a costume, they wouldn't want all of those heads popping out of doors seeing who was there. Why would someone go to all that trouble to put a sign on my door?

Most things in life, however, don't add up. That whole idea that the simplest story is the correct one isn't supported by facts on the ground. Life's complicated and messy. I needed to lighten up about the dark figure and wait to see if more notes appeared. So far, the suspense was fun.

At about four in the morning, the party was winding down. I dragged myself into bed and conked out.

37

"PRETTY BOY, SICK BIRD"

The damn trash trucks were out at six, and no one could sleep with all the banging dumpsters. I got out of bed, showered to wake myself up, and headed out to the diner where I met Fritz. He'd advanced me the money to pay the court fines. I had to tell him that Arbuckle would pay me soon. Then I could reimburse him. I also had to pay Johnny for his trouble. I asked Mabel for more stale donuts for later in the day. She said she would come through. Later on I would take them to the homeless shelter and visit Johnny.

Fritz and I went on to sneak in the back door of the crime lab. Narcissa was making another distracted circuit of the lab as we walked in. Here she comes. There she goes, Here she comes. There she goes. It must be tough being Narcissa, being so restless. Fritz asked her if the botulism was breaking out all over the city. She said that she didn't know. Narcissa asked if more graves were being added to the pet cemetery. I said it didn't seem so but I'd have to check it out. It began looking more and more like Muffin was a victim of some foul play.

We gave Narcissa the eagle sample. She ran her tests. She said, "No mistake about it. Botulism killed the eagle and it was the same strain that killed Muffin." Fritz and I smiled. It was likely that Alfie nailed Muffin, flew to the top of the tree, ate off her head, and then flew away. I asked Narcissa how long it would take for the eagle to topple over. She said that it would take an hour or two. There we had it. Fritz reminded me that he couldn't tell whether the dog remains were mutilated by an eagle. That is, when we took a peek at them in the cemetery. Muffin must've been poisoned, mutilated, and then Alfie whisked her off to the tree top.

Narcissa said, "Pretty boy, sick bird, pretty boy, sick bird. Te, he, he, he, Te, he, he, he."

Narcissa's black humor reminded me that I was supposed to make a doctor's appointment. Julie would quiz me on it later. I used Narcissa's phone and the receptionist wasn't friendly. I guess I owed some money from an earlier visit. Then the doctor came on, "Every time you come in your numbers are worse. You don't follow my advice. You shouldn't neglect your health."

I said, "Maybe I'm really sick and I need supplements or something."

That begrudging doctor, he made an appointment for a month from now. He was really worried about me. Don't worry Mr. de Loosher I'll hop on it a month from now. Well a month was fine with me. I wasn't crazy about seeing him too. He always looked down on how I lived. Didn't he hear about respecting a culture? You're supposed to respect it even though you don't like it. I have my own culture.

After the exam, he would do the drum roll. He put me in suspense, waiting for his prescription. Aw, same old, same old. He said the same thing about how I should live like he lives. This was followed by, Ka Ching, the ringing of the cash register. He charged too much, especially for saying the same thing he said last time. Here I go again. At least I was able to tell Julie that I made the appointment.

38

THE GRIFTER

Fritz and I returned to the museum where he had to make an appearance. After all, he was still on the job. His boss was this wiseacre named Freddy. He saw me come through the door and said, “Halloween man is back. What crypt did you crawl out of? He, he. Why do you work at looking so terrible?”

I said, “I’ll hold up a mirror to your face, and then you tell me why I look so bad.”

He saw that I wasn’t in a mood for ridicule. He said, “In all sincerity Jack, I’ve seen you look better than this.”

“I’ve been up most of the night. My apartment building erupted into this wild Dyngus Day party.”

“Probably all of that Polish food got to you.”

I told him that Polish pastry and beer were to die for. You could live on them. He went back to his sarcasm.

“You should get a couple of blood transfusions to bring back some of your color. Ha Ha.”

Fritz had to clean out some bird cages, so we talked as he wore space gear trying to scrub those dirty cages. I told Fritz that they should somehow let the birds fly over something to fertilize it. They are aerial fertilizing machines. Instead we’ve this terrible mess that has to be cleaned up again and again. Fritz said that it keeps him in work. We agreed that we would think about the mutilation and how we might go about proving how it was done. We would rendezvous for breakfast.

I now needed to do two things. I had to come up with some money to pay Johnny O and maybe Fritz if I could get enough. I had to get ready for dinner at Julie's. Arbuckle owed me money. I would start there.

Going back to her place was like going back to an abandoned building. As I already pointed out, people show off their life in what they display. Arbuckle had broken-down furniture and that was about it. I was looking for another angle to approach her.

As I passed the pet cemetery, I decided to check out if there were any new graves. There were quite a few, so I began taking an inventory of their head stones. Just as I started taking notes, guess who showed up.

"Plotting your next move Jack?" asked Lou.

"Lining up dinner?" asked Pete.

"You seem to be working on a menu from the fresh graves." said Lou.

"Knock it off guys. If you were half as hard on real criminals, there'd be no crime left in town."

Pete replied, "You need a season pass to the cemetery Jack."

"It's daylight, and I'm paying respects to these dearly departed animals."

"By eating them? Har. Har."

Pete couldn't resist getting his digs in.

"You guys give me the creeps."

"We're watching you Jack," Lou warned. "The judge didn't realize how weird you were. But we know. I feel sorry for Julie."

"Why do you guys hang out at the pet cemetery? You must have some childish fixation on dead pets."

With that, they left. What if all the newly buried pets had died from botulism? Could be. Let somebody else look into it. I was looking into Muffin's case because somebody was paying me. I went on to Arbuckle's. I didn't have time to call her. I sat in my car nearby and then got out to use a pay phone. Lo and behold, Arbuckle came from a basement apartment two doors down. She ditzed along with that big picture of Muffin under her arm. What in the world was she up to?

She went to her apartment. I began to smell a rat. I went to the basement flat and no one was there. I peeked in the window. The place was filled with pictures of all kinds of people and miniature stuffed dogs. There were even big stuffed dogs seated on chairs around the dining room table. I think I knew what was going on.

The managers of apartment buildings often lived in a basement apartment for free. Arbuckle used the other empty apartment as a shell place. She would transact business in the shell apartment. When it came time to pay, she would disappear back to the basement flat. I was about to be stiffed. She had set me up and who knows how many others. After my visit, I planned to watch her toddle back to her real place. Then I would surprise her. Corner her to get my money.

39

CATCHING THE CON

Arbuckle seemed happy to see me. She launched into caring and concern. She said that I looked thinner than before. With a big smile, she said that it looked like the wind would blow me over. That I should eat healthy food and get exercise. She said that she didn't believe what the awful police had to say about me. I didn't look like the sort of person who would eat poor Muffin or any other dog.

I chimed in that I had the dog specimen tested for poison. I put it that way rather than say I had a chunk of the dog tested.

"What happened?" she asked.

"The dog died from botulism in bad dog food."

"I'd never give the poor dog bad dog food."

"I didn't think you would. I don't think that anybody well-meaning would give her bad dog food either."

"You mean there was foul play?"

"It's on my radar screen."

As she asked about it, I kept my eyes on her eyes to see if she was sincere. She was convincing. What motive could she have for poisoning her own dog and afterwards hiring a private eye to discover what happened? It made no sense. With dead people, it may have been for insurance money or something like that.

"I'm about to fit more pieces into the puzzle. I need my first week's pay and an advance on week two."

She resisted my request. "Oh, I only have some cash with me."

I brought up my bill again. "I need a check for seven hundred dollars."

"I misplaced my check book. I'll give you my cash. When I find the check book, I'll pay you the rest."

"How much cash do you have?"

"Fifty dollars cash now and a check for the rest later. When the case is over, I'll give you a nice bonus."

I sensed that she had that line planned. While she seemed direct and simple, I was beginning to feel it all masked cleverness. How could she lose her checkbook in that empty place? She was pulling my chain.

"I need to eat too. Do you want me to drop the case?"

"No."

She teared up and said, "I miss Muffin. I want to know what happened to her."

I took the fifty dollars. It wasn't nearly what I needed to pay Johnny. I couldn't bring up last night's cemetery debacle about the eagle. She wouldn't want to pay for that. I went back to my car and waited. Sure enough. A short while later she came horizontally down the stairs and inched over to her real apartment. She did have great trouble walking. I waited a few more minutes and went to surprise her.

Ding dong.

"Why Miss Arbuckle, you have another apartment. I won't be long. Can I come in?"

"Why? I thought we were done for today."

She didn't know how to react to getting nailed. I pressed my way in. There on her cluttered dining room table was her checkbook. I walked over to it.

"I found your check book."

I peeked inside.

"Look, you have a healthy balance."

"Oh my gosh, there's the check book. Thank you for finding it."

She wrote the check for six hundred and fifty dollars.

She advised, "You better spend some of this money on food. I don't know why you would let yourself go like that. You should go to a spa, rest up, and eat like regular people."

As if in her rectangular world, she had an optimum shape. I told her she no longer needed to keep up the charade. She said that she didn't know what I was talking about.

I went to the diner to pick up the stale donuts. I was famished, so it was good to eat some glazed donuts for a snack. When I arrived at the shelter, most of the residents were gone for the day. You know, making rounds to various soup kitchens and charity organizations. There was always the park on a sunny day. I was told where I could find Johnny. He had this little pup tent where he kept his worldly belongings. It was hard to imagine that that big guy could get into that thing. He was sitting under a tree.

"Hey Johnny. Sorry about last night."

"I told you I didn't want to do anything wrong. Now I have to do community service. Are you going to pay me to do it?"

"Don't be sore Johnny. Sometimes things don't go according to plan."

"What a stupid idea. Do you have my money?"

"Here is the two hundred dollars. I don't know what to say about the community service. I'd pay you for doing it if I had the money. We're lucky that the judge thought you got stuck going into the cemetery rather than leaving it. Apart from admitting what we were up to, there's no case against us. You hadn't quite trespassed."

"Why don't you get a job to pay me for community service?"

"I have a job that doesn't pay well."

"Get another job. Pay me. Then we're square."

I told him I'd try to pay him minimum wage for the community service, but he didn't seem happy. I guess I just made one more thing in his life go bad.

I tried to smooth things over.

"It was a good plan that I had. Those cops weren't supposed to be staking out the cemetery. How was I to know?"

"The whole plan was to keep you guys off the hook. I was the fall guy. I'm glad you got caught Jack. You deserve it."

I thanked him for his help and said we'd be in touch.

40

PUTTING ON WATER

It was near dark when I got to Julie's. I was still in the doghouse from the night before. I give her credit. She stuck by me in court and all. As I walked in, I could tell she was simmering. Only one thing brings her to a boil: her weight. I started with a feeler of an opening.

"How was your day?"

She answered with, "The cops aren't such bad guys. You keep setting yourself up."

"Why are they on me like flypaper? They vegetate all day and come out of hibernation when they see me."

"But down deep, they're good guys. They try hard to interact with everybody. I think your bad health distorts your view of them. You don't see them for what they are."

I knew this was going nowhere. I changed the subject.

"Lab results showed that Alfie the eagle was also poisoned with botulism. Alfie ate some of Muffin when he flew to the top of a tree with the carcass."

Julie said that was progress and that Arbuckle would now want to pay me. I then filled her in that Arbuckle lived in another building and used the dusty place as a shell.

"Was she going to walk out on paying the final bill?"

I said I suspected that. I decided to corner her. I did and got my pay.

"Well, you can take me out to a movie or even ballroom dancing."

"I'm pretty well cleaned out. I had to pay Johnny, the court costs, and I owe Fritz the money he lent me."

"Do you have money for food?"

"I'll manage."

"You never seem to. If you skimp on anything, it's food. Did you make the doctor's appointment?"

"I did. He can't see me until next month."

"You may vanish by then."

She always picked on my weight when her weight was the issue. I knew it was coming. I thought it was no loss to go on the offensive.

"How is your diet coming?" I asked.

"I stepped on the scale and I'd gained two pounds. I could scream."

I now got to act understanding about it all.

"Maybe it's just water. Weight doesn't go on that fast. Believe me, I know."

"Why don't you put on water?" she asked.

"I try. The black coffee seems to prevent it."

"That's a thin excuse."

I brought it back to her. "Those little dinners you eat have got to be reducing your weight."

"Don't slip into the small dinners causing you to lose weight."

I now could play my trump card. "I showed you the big meals I had before I came over here. Look at this great plate of Polish food. Look at the after shot."

She seemed impressed. For a moment she believed that I was on the road to weight gain. The conversation went back and forth this way for some time. Ping, Pong. Ping, Pong.

Finally she lit the miserable candle, and we swallowed the morsels. I didn't want to ask her about cheating on her diet. Maybe she was sneaking calorie-rich foods— like fast food, carnival food, and drinks loaded with corn syrup. There was no point in starting that conversation. It would start and end on the wrong note.

We got on the subject of how Muffin became mutilated. She thought the poisoning and mutilation were connected. I said that it would take a foul beast to do that to a little dog. The players so far weren't beasts. Maybe the guy in the black trench coat is some maniacal dog-slasher. With that I went home to find another note on my door, "I WARNED YOU. NOW FACE THE MUSIC."

41

BEAUREGARD

I was exhausted. The note was threatening. It made sleep restless. Whatever was going on would reach a head soon. The neighbors were probably pulling my leg. What nut would dress in a trench coat to put a note on my door? "Face the music" and then some wise guy neighbor would blare the Pink Panther song on their stereo— got you that time Jack! Just thinkin', though, what if the dark stranger is a perp? I must've been getting close to the truth. But who could it be? Arbuckle and Blockman were immobile. Suppose I implicated one of them. There'd be no consequence. No law was broken. Did I smoke someone out and not know that I did? These thoughts kept going around and around in my brain— like Narcissa circling the lab.

I showered and got ready for the day. It's good being thin. The shower's short. You don't use much water. You save on soap too. You're more in harmony with the planet. There are more thin animals out there than heavy ones. Even Jungle Tom's gorillas are fit as a fiddle even though they just lounge around all day. I move around all day. That's why I'm thinner than the gorillas.

The new note brought the thought that the dark stranger was about to play his hand. I didn't have much of an idea about what kind of music I'd face. I did have an idea about breakfast.

I ate a couple of Dyngus-Day pastries and headed to the diner to meet Fritz.

Fritz had been thinking about the time line. Arbuckle let the dog loose in the park. Some time elapsed, enough time for the dog to be poisoned and mutilated. Alfie swooped down, grabbed the carcass, took it to the top of a tree, ate off the head and then flew home. For Fritz the question was, "Who poisoned the dog, who mutilated it, and are they the same person?"

Earlier in the investigation, I thought the dog might have been run over by the lawn mower. Suppose someone poisoned little Muffin. Her little tummy acted up. She staggered into the high grass. Her legs became rubbery and gave out. She collapsed. WHAM! The lawn mower runs over her. The driver wouldn't have seen her laying there the grass being high and all. Fritz said it seemed unlikely that the lawn mower guy would have poisoned the dog and then ran her over. Why mutilate the corpse? What did the lawn mower guy have against poor Muffin? Nothing. His role was accidental. He probably didn't realize it when he ran over her.

After I settled up with Fritz for the court fine, I gave Mabel a nice tip to keep her giving me stale donuts to take to the homeless shelter. We decided that our next step was to snoop around the maintenance area of the park. Afterwards, we would try to talk to the lawn mower guy. We didn't have to worry about the boys in blue. There they were, parked by the gate of the pet cemetery. That was their big chance to catch up on a few winks. I suppose I have myself to blame. I started the night owl grave digging. Now the town is running wild with rumors about goings-on at the cemetery. The owners should sell tickets. Give tours of the graves where it all began.

The maintenance shed was a large one with a number of pieces of equipment. The main lawnmower was like a tractor. The driver sat high in a cab with a wide set of blades set well in front of the cab. The accident that Fritz and I had in mind depended upon the grass being high enough where the collapsed dog wouldn't be easily seen by the driver. Now bear in mind that the dog had white fur so it would've been easy to spot if you were looking for it.

We hollered but the crew was out doing things around the grounds. There was a bulletin board behind the desk. That's where the head maintenance guy sat. The schedule of their assignments was blocked in day by day for the month. Fortunately, they didn't change the pack of sheets. We were able to sneak a peek of past months of when and who mowed the lawn. Sure enough, on the Thursday when Muffin met her fate, mowing was scheduled. The name "Beauregard" was penciled in. We checked the day's schedule to see where Beauregard was.

We found him on the south quarter trimming some shrubs. I asked him, "Mr. Beauregard, can we have a word with you?"

"Sure."

Now Beauregard was a tall guy. What was peculiar was that when he stood up, he thrust his jaw in the air. He didn't look down at us. He kind of rolled his eyes down to take a look at us.

"How can I help you fellas?"

"Remember last month when that little dog went missing and everyone was scouring the park to find it?" I asked.

"Strange day."

"Before the dog was reported missing, what were you and the crew working on?"

"Why do you want to know?"

"I'm working for the dog's owner who wants to understand what happened that day."

"Well, I started the day in tulip beds out front. I moved onto blowing leaves back into the wooded area. I then started edging the drive until the dog was reported missing."

Fritz then said that we were interested in grass cutting. Who was cutting grass that day?

"Oh, yeah. I think I did cut some grass that day. But I'm not sure. Maybe somebody else did the cutting. I don't remember."

I said that we saw the mower in the maintenance building and the cab was high. I asked about how easy it was to see what you were cutting.

"You get a very good view. You're high up."

Fritz said that the tractor seemed to have a sizable engine. It seemed pretty fast. He asked how fast it went.

"About four miles an hour. That baby really moves."

I asked about how tall the grass was that day. Beauregard said he didn't know. It all depended upon which grass was being cut. He said that some of it was tall. Some was short. It depended upon how the landscaper wanted to groom it. He then said, "Hey, you guys, what's this third degree all about?"

"Do you think you would have seen the little dog in the high grass?"

"Now wait a minute. If some poor little dog stepped in front of the lawn mower, any of us would have stopped right away. Are you accusing us of running over the dog?"

Fritz tried to calm him down. He said that we weren't out to blame anyone. We didn't care who did what. There wasn't a crime. We just wanted to know what happened. We wanted to put the dog owner's mind to rest.

Beauregard calmed down a bit. "I understand. None of us hit the dog. We would've known it. We would've stopped. Why in the world would we hit the dog and then climb a tree to put the dog up there? You answer me that one."

I said, "One way it could have gone is that the dog was mutilated by the lawn mower."

"You're barking up the wrong tree. All of us are careful. Are you trying to get us fired?"

I stressed to him that we weren't cops. I said that we think that if the dog was run over, it was dead already. He cautiously asked, "So, just sayin', somebody driving the mower would have hit a dead dog?"

"It could have happened that way."

As we walked to the car, Fritz thought Beauregard's answers were slippery when it came to who mowed the lawn that day. The schedule did say "Beauregard". His answers seemed too quick, like he'd already answered those questions to himself. He'd gotten ready for them. But maybe he didn't remember. He did seem to try to put blame on someone else. We both thought he had much more information about that day. He kept his answers short. He wanted to keep his job. He didn't want to snitch on anybody.

What we learned fit with Beauregard, his jaw in the air, barreling down on the poor dog. He mashed her but kept going. He realized that he might have hit something. He doubled back and found some blood. He began to worry. The dog found mutilated in the tree was a relief since no one would connect the mutilation with being struck by the mower. That's one way it could have gone.

42

THURSDAY

Fritz headed back to the museum. I tried to set out for Elysian Fields to visit Fanny Blockman. I set out but not for long. I had a flat tire. While changing the tire, I discovered a big nail that left a gaping hole. I dropped the tire off at the gas station. Maybe the flat tire was no accident. Somebody could have done a job on it. Was I "facing the music?" I would wait to see what Elmo at the garage had to say.

I wanted to mention to Fanny that Muffin had been poisoned— to gauge her response.

"Hi Fanny."

"You are that thin detective. Doesn't your doctor preach to you to gain weight? You look pale. You look anemic."

I then changed the subject. The exchange became interesting. I asked her if she ever got away from Elysian Fields. Did she take van trips to town. She answered, "Every Thursday the van takes a group of us into town to shop and do other things."

"Do you usually go with them?"

"It's Thursday today, and here I sit. Most weeks I'm feeling well enough to join them. Sometimes, like today, I can't move well enough. I like to go to shop or go to the park."

I then asked her if she was in town the day Muffin was killed.

"Yes, I was sitting on a park bench when people started

combing the brush looking for the poor dog. I tried to help but I couldn't go very far. I did look around the park bench a little."

I had her in the right time frame. Her memory seemed good. I asked her if she saw anything suspicious while sitting there.

"There were a lot of people in the park that day. Some buskers were by the plaza doing their acts. I was far away on a bench by one of the trails. I was there a few moments when people passed the word that the chubby dog was missing and they needed to search for it. I remember that I was trying to give some searchers some advice about places to look when we couldn't hear ourselves even though we were shouting. That maniac grass-mowing guy just roared on as if everything was normal."

A puzzle piece fit into place. Now on to the poisoning.

"You mentioned that when you had your dog Lily, you had a big bag of food for her?"

"A big bag. When she died, I kept some to treat the visiting dogs in the animal program."

"I think you said that you gave the rest to a neighbor?"

"Yes, that's right."

"Who was it?"

"It was that nice grey-haired man named Rufus. He liked to get out in his wheelchair and give dogs treats."

Fanny was both at the scene and seemed to have nothing to do with Muffin's death. The botulism-laced dog food behind the apartment down the hall could have been Fanny's. She could have given some to Muffin but it's unlikely.

In that big park, there was only an outside chance that Fanny would run into Muffin. She wouldn't know the food was poisonous. Chances were Fanny didn't poison Muffin. She could have, but most likely didn't. Besides, some of the rotten dog food still sits behind that apartment. It seemed undisturbed for a long time.

I said to her, "I discovered that Muffin died from botulism poisoning."

"How could such a thing happen?"

"I think she ate bad dog food."

"I knew Miss Arbuckle wasn't capable of taking care of that dog."

"It might've been an accident."

"Miss Arbuckle wouldn't deliberately poison Muffin. She loved that dog."

"That's why I suspect foul play. Muffin was poisoned in the park."

"Where would she find dog food in the park?"

I explained that someone must have given it to her. I was looking into that possibility. When I left, I told her I would keep her informed.

On my way back to town, I stopped at the garage, and asked Elmo about my tire.

"I ran over a nail. Huh Elmo."

"Looks that way. That's a mighty big nail. It would take a lot of hammering to drive that nail into the tire."

"You think somebody did that?"

"Naw. You ran over it."

Elmo placed just enough doubt in my mind. I couldn't rule out vandalism. Lou and Pete didn't like me. They didn't dislike me enough to do all the work of hammering a nail in my tire. After that job they would've been through for the day. I was lost for who might do such a thing.

43

FACING THE MUSIC

I was on my way home to get ready for Julie's. Just daydreaming along. As I was walked past the apartment building next to mine, KA BOOM, a large paving stone crashed to the sidewalk right behind me. It took a moment for the fear to set in. It hit so hard that it cracked the pavement. My reflex was to look up. I didn't see anyone. What a close call. Whew! I could've been killed. That's how Cyrano de Begerac died— a paving stone. They couldn't kill him fair and square, in a sword fight, so he met fate with that paving stone. I'm not saying that I'm a Cyrano. Actually no one was Cyrano. He's a fictional character.

I was so shook up, I called 911 and some cops were sent. Guess who showed up? Of course, the cops with nothing to do.

Lou said, "Almost got you huh Jack. There must've been three or four guys on top of this building, just aiming to crush you. Ha. Ha."

Pete joined in. "They would have to be a good shot. You're two-dimensional! That's a good one!"

"Very funny. If you guys take off your clown hats, and be serious for a minute, I'm getting paranoid. Today, I had a bad flat tire that could've been vandalism. I had threatening notes taped to my door."

"What did they say, 'Don't eat the dead dog. It's poisoned.'? That's funny!"

"Have your fun. I want you guys to put these things on record. Just in case something happens to me, you won't be clueless."

Pete said, "Look buddy, we'll be on the lookout for some old ladies chasing you with a butcher knife."

With that they burst into laughter.

I said, "Look at those jelly rolls bounce. You guys burn a lot of calories when those big guts bounce around. You can thank me for making you laugh. I'm helping you lose weight."

I'd hoped that some other police would've shown up. There were some really good police on the force. They knew how to do an investigation. My guys would write the wrong things down. Fill the report with fantasies about my motives and not have a clue as to what to do next. If someone does me in, put it in the unsolved murders file.

"We'll keep an eye on your apartment shamus. We seem to be protecting you even though we don't want to. You're our major source of crime. Hearty har har."

"I just want something on the record. If this paving block wasn't an accident, there'll be more accidents around the corner."

44

AXE TROUBLE

After I showed the boys the notes and filled them in, I didn't want to tempt fate and hang around at the apartment. I went to visit Fritz at the museum to catch him up. On the way I got this banana split at The Frozen Palace. You can choose your toppings. I loaded on seven of them. I won't go into them all, but you know what I mean. Those things keep you full for hours. Fritz was on his lunch hour and had time to talk.

"Things seem to be coming to a head with me as the target. I'd a very bad flat tire when I went out to my car, and I was just about home when a paving block fell from the roof and nearly got me."

"You think it was related to those notes?"

"One thing followed on the heels of the other. I called the cops to get it all on record. Unfortunately, our buddies Lou and Pete took the report."

"You gave them a description of the guy in the trench coat?"

"Yeah, they took that down. They said that they would keep an eye on my place."

He asked about who might be going after me. All that I could come up with was that crazy lawn mower guy. He wouldn't have much to do with the dog however."

Fritz said, "What about Johnny O? He was pretty pissed."

I said, "Johnny's a good guy. He's an old buddy from my tramp steamer days. Besides he doesn't have a trench coat."

Fritz said that it seemed to him that Johnny wasn't the sort to sneak around making threats. He thought Johnny couldn't care less about the dog. He thought it quite a leap from the notes to the paving block. If that's how it was going, the next move might be curtains.

I told him that's why I decided not to hang around the apartment. If I knew what I was up against, I could defend myself. I asked if there was anything we overlooked.

"We didn't look into the eagle's owner. Maybe he's angry about the dog poisoning his eagle?"

I said, "Naw, his eagle plopped over. He didn't know that the poisoned dog was responsible. Besides, it wasn't my dog and I didn't poison it."

I thanked Fritz for being a big help. He reminded me that the tire and paving block might have been coincidences. "Don't make too much of them. The notes might be just some prankster."

I said I'd like to think that. I headed back to the apartment to clean up before going to Julie's.

When I got to my door, OH MY GOSH, there was a fireman's axe embedded in the door. The pointed side was in the door with another note. "YOU ARE GOING TO GET YOURS." I called 911 and the dispatcher sent out the boys.

"Why does Jack live on the third floor. These steps are killing me."

"Yeah Lou, Jack should give us a commendation for risking a heart attack."

"He shouldn't make it so hard to get police protection."

"Hay Jack, hay Jack. Meet us half way."

I peeked in the well in the middle of the stairs.

"You've got to come all the way up. You've got to see this."

When they got to the door, they saw my "Here's Johnny" moment— you know, like Jack Nicholson with the axe going after Shelley Duvall in "The Shining."

Lou said, "WOW, somebody's wrecking private property!"

Pete added, "They're going to pay for this. You can't just go around wrecking people's doors."

"Do you fine officers take this as a death threat?" I asked.

"I don't know. He doesn't say he's going to kill you. What is 'getting yours' to you Lou?"

"I don't know. Whatever someone owes you."

"Come on guys, he isn't going to write me a big check or something."

"You think this has something to do with the little dog?" Pete asked.

I said that the first two threatening notes were about the dog. That jogged their memories. A skeptical Lou asked,

"You think the notes are related?"

Pete thought a moment and said, "Yeah, some could be pranks and then this serious dude comes along with the axe."

"I'll show you guys the notes again."

They gawked at the notes. In his expert, official voice Lou said, "Yep, looks like the same handwriting."

Pete added, "Don't worry Jack, there's going to be no more vandalism on our watch."

I said sarcastically, "I'm glad my apartment has nothing to worry about."

"Well if he comes after you, just turn sideways and he won't be able to see you. Ha Ha."

45

MORE PLOTS, MORE CASH

I went right over to Julie's to tell her about the danger. I didn't want her to get caught off guard. I needed to pick her brain for ideas. When I arrived her eyes had this rather distant look. I couldn't put my finger on it. As she began talking, I got the feeling that she was talking about the diets. She seemed to be saying that I'm a pathetic, hopeless case.

"You should see a doctor soon. You're eating well and still losing weight. Something serious must be going on."

I said to her that it was just the "same old, same old." She didn't think so. I said what I'd usually say, that no matter what I ate, I didn't gain weight. Sometimes I even lost some.

I knew that my eating habits were going to catch up with me. On the plus side, I made it this far. Right? I went back into the fact that I've a high metabolism. She then said I had this "pasty and oily" look. I hadn't noticed a change in my look. Even my look had gone bad. What's left? Maybe she knows better. Maybe her intuition is telling her something. Maybe I'm about to tip into a coma or something.

I said, "I do need better nutrition. What I don't understand is that I started to lose weight when you hid the junk food."

"Don't give me that one. More junk food and you would be healthy as a horse. Right."

"I'm just sayin' that the new diet is when all of this weight loss began to happen."

"Just like you, to blame a better diet. You only lost two pounds."

Phew! I managed to turn it around. Only two pounds now! When we started two pounds was a catastrophe. Heh, Heh. With that I decided not to push my luck. I changed the subject to the mortal peril that I was in. I could see she had that "Poo, Pah," attitude about my mortal peril until I got to the axe in the door.

"My God, you don't want someone chasing you with an axe!"

I confessed that I was trying to get my head around the problem but was lost for ideas. I asked her who she thinks is the homicidal maniac.

She said, "With the first note, you know that it has something to do with the dog. With the last message, you know you must be getting close to flushing someone out. He's out for blood."

She was right. But who?

I told her that Fritz went through the list of suspects. Unless one of them hired the loony-tunes with the axe, I'd no idea what they wanted.

While talking, I was fumbling around in my pockets. I found the list of freshly buried dogs at Heaven's Rest. I showed the list to Julie. She said, "Look at these names."

There I saw Buttercup, Ditsy, Arf-Arf, Horse, Bowser, Cuddles, and Pee Wee.

"Well so what?"

"They're all names of cute little dogs."

Sure enough. They were the kind that are chubby and that the rectangular sort of older ladies like.

The older-ladies idea struck me. They're the ones that would put up the money for burying a dog in the cemetery. Most normal people would say a few respectful words and then dispose of the body. The big ladies go all out.

Julie said, “That’s what I’m thinking Jack. More dogs to bury, more business. The owner of the pet cemetery stands to gain. You were onto the dog poisoning. The owner wants you out of the way.”

Julie made good sense. I didn’t even know who owned the cemetery. It was a good lead.

46

THE BELLY AND THE CANNON

When I arrived back near my apartment building, the street was swarming with cop cars. There was Tony handcuffed to someone. Yo! Yo! I did a double take. That someone was in a trench coat and had on a black broad-brimmed hat. Pete saw me, "Jack, we caught the vandal. You're lucky you didn't run into her."

"What do you mean 'her?'"

"The perp is Meadowlark Merriweather. She kept calling us to keep grave robbers away from her cemetery."

"You mean she's the owner of Heaven's Rest?"

"Yeah. She had this cannon with her— the most powerful handgun in the world."

"She was out for blood?"

"You got that right. Fortunately, she didn't realize that you didn't have much blood."

"Very funny Pete."

Pete started the story. "We sat there in our squad car, and all of a sudden, she popped out of the shadows and tried to get into the building. Before anyone let her in, Lou and I managed to corner her in the vestibule. She's a mean one and strong as an ox. Lou grabbed the gun and got it away from her. He's a real hero. She would have shot both of us. We had enough police there to subdue her. She kept making threats against you."

Lou said, "I don't know what you did to her Jack, but she was out for your ass."

"You're going to lock her up, aren't you?"

"Sure, but we have her on the vandalism charge, pulling a gun on us, and the threats. I think she'll be out on bail before you know it."

Pete said, "I'll talk to the prosecutor about keeping her locked up. She shouldn't be out on bail. The judge, though, may just issue a restraining order against her. An ankle bracelet won't stop that one. She'll rip it off her ankle and make you choke on it."

I pressed them that they had to keep her in jail longer. I told them I needed time to build a better case against her. Lou said he would put a good word in for me. That left it wide open. She might be let out tonight or kept in jail for a while. They said nothing that I could count on. I had to get busy.

Then Pete said, "Like what sort of case? You didn't let us in on it." I said that I didn't know myself but I knew how to find out. "Good work guys."

I was trying to leave when officer Angelo Porcini, better known as "The Mushroom," trapped me.

He said, "I was right in on it Jack. I'll fill you in."

I said, "Ok, Angelo."

"When we saw her about to enter the building, we rushed the door. Lou and Pete got in, but there was no room for me. So, I was holding the outside door open. Just when we cornered her, she pulled out the cannon. There wasn't time to be afraid. I could see that she was so agitated she could've shot all of us. I reached for my radio to call backup, my hand slipped and the door began to slam shut. The plunger in that door was really powerful. The door hit Pete in the backside. This threw him off balance, and he fell into Lou. I heard this great "OOF" sound. He was like a sumo wrestler slamming someone from behind. Pete's belly smashed into Lou. Lou was thrown off balance. He fell into the woman, catching her arm with his big belly. It pinned her arm against the wall. She groaned. AUGH! Lou grabbed the gun. He was a real hero."

After Angelo's story, I had a sudden realization. Those big bellies were part of Lou's and Pete's arsenals. They were real weapons. Thank goodness for those weapons. If they hadn't cornered Merriweather in the vestibule, she would've been long gone. Give credit to the boys. Without their action, I would've had an ambush waiting for me. A quick kill and no one would have been the wiser. Her big mistake, according to the boys, was destroying private property.

47

THE MAGNIFICENT SEVEN

It was into the wee hours, but I was too worked up to sleep. I went back to Julie's to plot strategy. She was relieved that my assassin was caught. I said that we needed to get the goods on Merriweather. The way to do it was to prove that the dogs in the seven recent burials were poisoned with the same botulism. To do that, we needed to get samples from those dogs.

We had to go back to the pet cemetery, dig up the coffins, and with our steak knives, take a chunk from each dog for Narcissa to test. Julie said she saw the logic in my plan, but it was crazy to go back there and especially dig up seven graves. If I were caught, Lou and Pete would be hysterical that I was dining on dogs, and they would lock me up.

We thought long and hard about it over cans of pop. We concocted a plan. She would invite Lou and Pete over to her place for a hero's dinner. She would make excuses for me saying that I would be late. But I couldn't take the amount of time needed to dig up all of those graves. I needed help. It would go faster with help. It would go very fast with more help. Julie suggested I invite six friends and that each would dig up a grave. Excellent plan. My friends knew about poor Muffin and would volunteer to stop that maniac Meadowlark from poisoning any more poor little dogs.

We worked on a list: Andre the pet groomer, Jungle Tom, Birdman Fritz, Narcissa, Mabel from the diner, and Johnny O. I stayed overnight at Julie's and contacted them in the morning. After I explained the plan and the fact that it was an emergency, five of them agreed to help. Johnny resisted because there was nothing in it for him being homeless and all. I played up the fear angle quite a bit and Johnny agreed for old times' sake.

All of them didn't want to see the mad woman firing the cannon at yours truly or chasing him down the street with an axe. As Mabel said, "One for the Jack-o-lantern." Julie then called the station to speak to Lou. He was excited about recognition as a hero. He and Pete would go to Julie's after dark. I was supposed to join them after looking into the case a bit more.

We assembled at the diner. We couldn't stand around very long because Narcissa was fidgeting, Jungle Tom repelled everyone with his stench, Andre was making the diner smell like a pet grooming studio, and Johnny O with a little time would have wanted to back out. I was bringing in the shovels and steak knives when Jungle Tom snatched my list of cute dead dogs. He took command.

"We have to be in and out in half an hour, tops. There'll be no time to get organized once in the cemetery. Each of you'll have a pet to dig up."

Tom had led expeditions into the jungle and his bossy style was showing. It was getting the job done.

"Ok, Andre, you take Cuddles. Mabel, you take Buttercup. I'll take Arf-Arf. Johnny O, you take Horse. Jack, you've got Pee Wee. Narcissa you've got Bitsy, and Fritz, you've got Bowser."

Already the group was restless, and Narcissa began circling the room.

"Go right to your little dog's grave, dig it up, open the vault, and with your steak knife lop off a chunk."

"Steak knives make such a ragged cut. I brought a scalpel."

"That's fine Narcissa. Now Mabel gave you a carry out carton. Label it with your dog's name. Here are some pens. After you take your specimen, seal it up."

Narcissa continued, "When you are done, give the cartons to me. Close the vault and rebury it, Te, he, he, he, Te, he, he, he."

I then said, "Make sure you try to leave the grave as undisturbed-looking as possible. And Johnny, you are the tallest. Take this pole, sneak up on the surveillance camera. Turn it away from the entrance so that we can all slip in. When leaving we quickly go our separate ways, trying not to attract attention."

Fritz asked, "Where'll Lou and Pete be during all of this?"

"They'll be at Julie's apartment having an appreciation dinner. I'll join them no later than ten."

Narcissa said, "I'll work through the night until I test all of the samples. I'll let Jack know the results and he'll contact you."

We gave Johnny a head-start so he could redirect the camera. He was leery about being the first one there. If he were caught moving the camera, it would all be on his head while we would scatter and leave him holding the bag. Lucky for us, he was the strong silent type, so he just halfheartedly went along with the plan. We decided to approach Heaven's Rest from different directions so as not to attract attention. The problem was that we were all carrying shovels and flashlights. Most people driving by, though, seemed like they couldn't care less. We all made a quick turn into the cemetery. So far, so good.

I led the group to the gravesites and set them loose. If anyone was watching the cemetery, we stood out like sore thumbs. And we made quite a racket. The aim was to make it a quick racket. Then a quiet sadness settled over us as we saw a tiny grave, a tiny vault, and a little corpse. It made me angry to think that this was a cutie pie named Pee Wee. He couldn't hurt a fly. The thought of his days cut short by poison. Only to sell that lousy burial plot. Andre resisted using his steak knife, so Narcissa took a piece of Cuddles with her scalpel and put it into a carton for him.

Mabel brought along two carry-out bags from the diner. We put the cartons from the pets into the bags. Narcissa was off to the lab. If the boys in blue had searched Narcissa's bags, their eyes would've bugged out.

48

THE HEROES' DINNER

I hurried to Julie's to join the party. When I arrived, Lou waved his arm at me like he didn't want to be interrupted. He was in the middle of bragging about how he didn't hesitate and grabbed the gun. Pete encouraged him to tell the story and talked about his role getting the cuffs on her. I added that Angelo, "The Mushroom," got her in a headlock while this was going on.

"I suppose Angelo did that. I don't know how there could've been room for him to get behind her."

I decided to stay polite.

"Angelo said you guys moved forward so he could get in."

"That's it. Pete and I moved right in on her. I managed to trap her gun-hand against the wall. That way she couldn't shoot us, and I could take the gun away from her with my other hand. If that cannon had gone off in the vestibule, we would all be deaf today."

"Hey you guys, there's bravery in the line of duty. You rose to the occasion. Lou the lion hearted." OK, I was laying it on thick.

"Thanks again guys for saving me from the ambush."

"We were lucky she was trapped in that vestibule. We could've had quite a gun battle with her cannon going off."

Julie proposed a toast. "Here's to Lou and Pete, police

heroes, who saved the day and many lives."

We all raised our cans of pop and took a drink. The boys were beaming.

"From the bottom of our hearts, Pete and I would like to thank you for this fine tribute and dinner. I knew down deep that at least you Julie appreciated our efforts."

He was trying to make me feel small again. I smoothed over the dig.

"Forget our rough patches, especially recently. When the chips are down and it's time to act, you guys don't flinch and meet the call. Another toast to the boys in blue."

We drank again, and then Julie brought on the dinner.

Julie went all out. What a feast. For an appetizer, we had this big bowl of marshmallows roasted on the grill. You should've seen the guys dig in. She then cooked up some chuck steaks from the freezer. They still looked real good. They were a little over-cooked. I like a little charcoal crust. They were kind of hard to chew. We had plenty of time though. Julie oiled the works with as much ketchup as we needed. With the steaks we had this big bowl of potato chips fresh out of the bag.

For a veggie she boiled up some okra. I don't particularly like okra. When you boil it, it turns slimy. It'll make you sick seeing someone taking it from the pot. She slathered it with butter and sour cream. I went light on the okra.

The boys thought everything was wonderful. We topped the whole shebang with another can of pop and two-dozen delightful cup cakes with generous layers of white frosting.

The guys ate so fast that they finished a dish before Julie could bring on the next. Can those guys eat. There was nothing left. In Angelo's story, their most lethal weapon was their bellies. They were keeping those lethal weapons in shape. Preserving their gravity, their mass so to speak. Pity the next armed perp having to face that belly.

I was relieved that Julie came up with some normal food. I was starving. I didn't get a chance to eat since the morning. I have to admit I have kind of a sweet tooth. I have to get serious about looking better before that doctor's appointment.

Out of clear blue, Lou said to me,

"You once called me a slush gut. Well that's not right." He stood up, put his hands all the way around to the front of his belly and said,

"Do you want to know how much money I spent on food developing this baby? Do you know how many pork roasts and barbeque chickens it took? I want you to feel this."

"What am I supposed to feel?"

"Just feel it. You too Julie."

It was hard as a rock. No fat there. On the other side of that abdominal wall was another world. Heaven forbid. You'd find a sea of fat with a cavern in the middle for a stomach.

"I have to admit, that isn't a slush gut," while pointing to it.

"See. Not that I'm trim or anything. You have to admit that I've the core of an athletic build."

With that I choked up. My eyes filled with tears and I was about to burst. One of the hardest things I ever did was hold back that explosion. Julie had a broad grin. Even Pete looked pale with his mouth open. Lou's weapon probably cracked a couple of Merriweather's ribs. That's why she let go of the gun.

"Well, you could stand to lose a few pounds. You and Pete should join in Julie's diet program. We'll weigh you guys in tonight. I'll get the scale."

Julie smirked a little.

Lou spoke up, "The time has to be right to start a diet. It's mostly psychology. You have to be in the right frame of mind."

Pete added, "I was on a diet and it was too rigid. When that happens, it doesn't last long."

I didn't want to push it. This was a special night. Having a little sport was ok. Rancid talk wasn't.

We settled into an after-dinner treat. Julie had been hiding the double layer box of milk chocolate buttercreams. You can't just eat one. By the end of the box, we were ready to scream and bounce off the walls.

The boys asked me what Merriweather had against me. I told them that I tested the dog sample that was in my fridge. It had botulism in it. It seemed someone poisoned a dog with bad dog food. I kept talk of Muffin out of it. My fridge sample was supposed to be from some other dog. I told them that the poisoning was no accident. Probably Merriweather was the culprit. She threatened me with the notes on my door. I was supposed to drop the case.

Pete said, "Poisoning a dog is only a misdemeanor."

Julie countered, "There are many more poisoned dogs. Their owners are sentimental and bought plots in Heaven's Rest."

Lou said, "It's hard to believe that she was doing that under our noses. It's hard to believe. We saw her a couple of times a day. She loved the dead little dogs."

Pete tried to put it together. "We were helping protect her by guarding the graves. She's a criminal. You're a criminal too Jack. The judge found you guilty."

I took them back to the court hearing. I reminded them that I was only guilty of helping Johnny get his feather.

Pete said, "Nice work figuring things out Jack."

Lou said, "Call us if you need help."

They never caught on that their dinner was to keep them out of the way.

49

THE PLAN

After Lou and Pete left, I filled Julie in on the Magnificent Seven's dig. We seemed to have gotten away without a hitch. I needed to clean up, get the dirt from under my nails, and sleep. I told Julie my first stop in the morning was Narcissa's lab. We were closer to each other, Julie and I, now that we worked together on the case. I thought I had at least one more day to come up with the evidence I needed.

When I got back to the apartment, there were still lights on all over the building. Crime scene tape was all over the place. I had to enter the building from the rear. The axe, the notes, the dark figure, the cannon, the cops. There was much for the neighbors to talk about. I tried to avoid them. I slept soundly having a full meal to sleep on.

I got up at daylight. I had a lot to do. I headed to Narcissa's lab. There she was, moving here and there, even after her all-nighter.

"Good news. Or even bad depending on what you want. Te, he, he, he. Te, he, he, he."

I could cut the suspense with a knife. She was building suspense in her usual nervous way.

"Six of the seven dogs were poisoned with the same strain of botulism. Only Horse wasn't."

I said to Narcissa that that's great news. Six out of seven

is plenty of evidence. I said I owed her one for staying up the night to run the tests.

"I couldn't sleep anyway. Too much tension. I don't like pacing the floor rather than sleeping."

"Yeah, pacing keeps the neighbors up. You know, in the jail cells below the lab. But, there's an upside." I was trying to be positive. "Pacing's good exercise."

She said, "No, no, Jack. When I pace, I'm applying my method. I always look for patterns. A pattern shows the general case."

"I should start thinking like you Narcissa."

"What are you going to do with the evidence Jack?"

I told her I'm meeting Birdman Fritz at the museum to discuss strategy.

"I would get on this quickly, Jack, while everyone is worked up. Right now, they feel how vicious this Meadowlark Merriweather was."

"Good point Narcissa." I thanked her again for her big- time effort.

"I wouldn't have missed the exhumation for the world."

I met Fritz outside the owl exhibit. He was working on refreshing the owl nests. He told me that owls were fierce predators. To me, they looked so innocent. They're half asleep on their perches. It's like they wouldn't hurt a fly. You'd have to poke one to get a response. Fritz advised not doing that.

He said that once they go into attack mode, you better not be on the receiving end. They demand respect. I mentioned to Fritz that to the boys in blue, Merriweather was like that. Once she was out to get me, she was a force of nature.

I filled in Fritz about the lab results. We agreed that none of the evidence from Muffin's sample or from the raid would count in court. He reminded me that the main case was on her for menacing, for almost killing Lou, Pete, and Angelo.

I had my plan. I had the evidence. The same evidence lies buried in the cemetery. All the prosecutor had to do was figure out how to legally go back to the graves and get it.

Fritz liked the idea. The police would interview the owners of the dead dogs and say there was evidence of foul play. The owners would give permission for exhumations. That evidence would be legal.

"I hope it works that way, fingers crossed."

The trick was to keep Merriweather out of the way. Fritz said, "You better hide if she's set free." Then I started to think mushy out loud. Maybe her attitude would improve. Maybe she would've realized that the jig was up. Maybe she would get ahold of herself and reform.

"That's enough 'ifs' even to choke a theologian."

"I never tried to choke a theologian. Now I know how."

I added that Merriweather acted like such a maniac that a judge wouldn't just put her back on the street. She's so dangerous, it shows that she's incompetent. A court psychiatrist should get involved. Fritz said I should suggest that to the prosecutor. Hold her 'for observation and evaluation' while building the rest of the case.

I headed over to the prosecutor's office to plant some ideas.

50

PROSECUTOR JACKSON

The prosecutor for this case was this tough old bird Tamara Jackson. She was a defense attorney turned prosecutor. She was old enough to have seen it all. As I walked into her office, she said that she'd been waiting to talk to me. She wasn't sure about what additional charges to bring against Merriweather. I told her that's why I was there.

"How old are you young man?" she asked.

"I'm thirty-five."

"I must say you look much over sixty. Are you in bad health?"

Now that was dishonest for starters. She saw I was young. If she thought I was over sixty, she wouldn't have brought it up. Who would ask someone who is over sixty whether they're over sixty? It was an excuse to do what they always do. They bring up that health thing. As if they were so concerned. I played coy.

"Not that I know of."

"Your color is terrible. You should seek help."

"I've heard that before."

"Do you listen to gospel music?"

"No. I don't listen to much music."

"Gospel will inspire you to take steps. You need to take steps young man."

While trying hard to disregard her comments, I noticed that she had this big picture, a painting, of a great golden eagle above her desk.

"You like eagles?"

"I do. I used to have a pet eagle."

"How long ago?"

"He died recently."

The light bulb went on, "Was his name Alfie?"

"How did you know?"

I told her that Merriweather owns Heaven's Rest pet cemetery. I was investigating the mysterious death of a poor little dog named Muffin. Alfie's grave was right next to Muffin's.

"You are observant," she said.

I said that I couldn't miss her big eagle sculpture. It loomed over all of those tiny graves— the tiny graves of the little dogs.

"I know that someone is going to steal the sculpture sooner or later. It is worth quite a lot of money. I didn't have the heart to keep it in my garden. I moved it to the cemetery as a tribute to Alfie."

I brought up that I gathered some evidence to prove that Muffin died of botulism found in dog food. I suspected that after Muffin died, Alfie ate some of Muffin. She didn't seem surprised.

"So, you think that's why she just up and toppled from her perch?"

I said, "If I may be so bold, I think you let her out for exercise. She saw the dead Muffin. Ate some of her. Flew home. And died."

She got a bit huffy. She said I had no evidence for that. I back-tracked quickly. I was an idiot for accusing the prosecutor of anything. I said I honestly wasn't suggesting any wrong doing on her part. That I was just speculating how Alfie might have died. Purely hypothetical.

She asked how I could prove that Merriweather poisoned

Muffin. I cut to the chase that I thought she'd poisoned several dogs the same way in order to sell burial plots.

She was firm. "We'll have to stop her."

I let her in on the backstory. I said, "You aren't supposed to know this, but I managed to test Muffin and those several dogs and seven out of eight of them died from botulism."

She asked for my evidence of dog poisonings. I told her I could give her a lab report. The problem was that it was obtained illegally. I said that I wouldn't say how in order not to incriminate myself. She asked what I proposed.

I went into it. "Gather your own lab results and build your case. The little bodies should be exhumed and tested for botulism. All the while you know from my lab results what the tests will show."

She said it would be difficult to start the case from scratch. The other charges against Merriweather were low-hanging fruit that didn't require much police work. She asked how much the police knew. I told her that they didn't know much— only what I'd told them. They'd need to do fresh investigating.

I knew that was the kink in my plan. Lou and Pete would be put to work on the case. It would be on the slow track to nowhere. Give those guys a deadline and they fall asleep. I was counting on Jackson. She had a bee in her bonnet. She lost an eagle and indirectly Merriweather was at fault. It wouldn't take gospel music to put a fire under her.

Jackson said, "Very clever. All of this will take time."

I appealed to her about my safety. Merriweather acted like a maniac and tried to kill police as well as me. While the case was being worked on, she should be up for psychiatric evaluation.

She thought it was worth trying. "I have to warn you, though, our police force is very busy and we have to investigate felonies before what appears to be a misdemeanor."

I thought to myself, "Yeah, the boys in blue lead hectic lives. They keep a lid on the city. They're the thin blue line.

Well, maybe it's now a thick blue line— at least their part of it."

As you can see, the meeting with prosecutor Jackson couldn't have gone better. I contacted the team about the good news. We were on our way to solving this case. Justice would be served. But I was finished with my part. No more pay, no more work. Pass the baton to the police. Merriweather had a court appearance the next day. I would be there to see what she looked like in the flesh without her costume. Julie and Fritz wanted to join me.

51

THE HEARING AND "NIAGARA FALLS"

The hearing opened with the accused being asked whether she was innocent or guilty of the charges. They included damaging private property, menacing, stalking, and resisting arrest with intent to kill. She pled not guilty. Then she turned around and saw me. She got this fierce look in her eyes. She lunged for an officer's gun, missed taking it, and charged toward me shouting, "I'm going to kill you, you dog eater." Fritz got in front of me before she could claw at me. It was awful. The judge declared her a danger and ordered a psychiatric evaluation. I didn't know that I could bring out such hostility in anyone.

Julie said we should move to another state before they let her out. I thought that she'd better show hostility when the psychiatrist evaluated her. If I'm her only trigger, then everyone else would think she's as normal as green grass. That is, until she sees me, and KER BLAM! I'm fighting for my life.

I told Julie her outburst seemed like the deranged guy in the Abbott and Costello movie. Every time the guy heard the words "Niagara Falls," he relived a terrible incident where he strangled someone. Upon hearing Abbot say "Niagara Falls", he slowly approached Costello and began strangling him. Abbott coyly lets the words slip out again and again. Each time Costello sees Abbot about to say the words, he tries to stop him. He knew the guy was going to fly off the handle again.

Julie said that the psychiatrist needed a trigger like "Niagara Falls." Hmmm. What about a picture of me? Whenever the psychiatrist thought Merriweather had recovered, she would flash my picture and Merriweather would go bonkers. I'd no idea what a triggering photo would look like. With the Polaroid camera, Julie took a picture of me just like I was in court. That should do the job. I made sure the psychiatrist had it before interviewing Merriweather.

52

CALM AND STORM

Things were going so well that I began to feel uneasy. Things just couldn't be going that well. My life isn't charmed. Something bad must be around the corner. Julie was happy. I exchanged the usual jabs with Lou and Pete. I solved the case for the most part. I owed Johnny O some money, but that was about it. All of this seemed too good to be true. Living happily ever after just seemed wrong. That happened only in fairy tales. As usual, I tried to figure out what could go wrong next. As usual, I was lost for what that might be.

I had a lot to report to Arbuckle. Since the case was over and I'd been successful and she had the money, I could get the rest of my pay and move on. I tried to call her. It wasn't a working number. Suspicions flooded my mind. I was ready for a fight. I went to her apartment. She had moved out. I went to the owner of the building. She was angry that Arbuckle had stiffed her for utilities and loans. She had no idea where Arbuckle had gone.

I went to Elysian Fields. They'd been trying to find her. She owed them a ton of money. They didn't know about the dusty apartment. They had no forwarding address. Everybody had the same story. They said if I should find her, to let them know. The lady was a lousy grifter. Damn.

I should have gotten all of my pay when I cornered her checkbook and saw she had plenty of money. That woman can hardly move. How did she just disappear? She's a sharpie. Why didn't she want to know the latest on Muffin? Wasn't it worth the money? What was her game? Pay for nothing and not get caught? Her game certainly wasn't to fatten me up.

Later in the day as I was walking down the street, Lou and Pete pulled up.

"Hey you walking stiff. You look more like a corpse than ever. On the grave yard shift again Jack."

"You two sorry sacks of foul gas. Don't light a match anywhere near you two. What're you up to? Persecuting law-abiding citizens again?"

I could tell from their expressions that they weren't in a jovial mood. Lou had this nasty, serious look on his face.

"Did you see the paper Jack? Your crime ring was at it again. That big guy with black hair was spotted with a shovel and a pole near the cemetery."

With that they drove off.

My heart sank. News media played up the story about Johnny being stuck on the cemetery fence and all. They connected it to me almost being shot dead. Somebody must've seen Johnny with the shovel the night the Magnificent Seven did some digging. I went to the newsstand, bought a pack of cigarettes and some juju beans. As I was popping the beans, there on the front page was the story. It wasn't a headline, but you still couldn't miss it.

A number of good citizens spotted a number of people with shovels. They were converging on the pet cemetery like water swirling down a drain. Johnny was identified because TV media spread his image from the fence debacle. I was worried about me because of all the pictures on TV of the private investigator that ate dead pets.

Now Lou and Pete were going ballistic. And after Julie's hero's dinner. Some gratitude. So much for peace-making. I knew just how their minds worked. They were thinking that the caper was all about grave robbing. The grave robbers used the investigation as a cover. The dead pet gourmets must be stopped. Look out, here comes all sorts of stuff hitting the fan. Here comes the weight of the world. I got my shoulders ready.

I headed over to the museum to talk to Fritz. I told him what the boys said and about the newspaper article. In court, Merriweather accused me of eating dead dogs. She didn't say she was going to kill me because I exposed her dog-poisoning scheme. Where in the world did she get the idea of eating dead dogs?

"Fritz, I think I know where Merriweather got the business of me eating dead pets. Lou and Pete brought that up when they invaded my apartment. They went right to the refrigerator. They put the thought in her head."

"You're wrong Jack. It looks like they invaded your place to 'look for' evidence that you robbed a grave and were about to eat what you stole."

"So you're saying Merriweather gave them that idea?"

"Makes sense."

The boys were almost working just for her. That's how they were spending a lot of their time. She kept on them. They're empty urns waiting to be filled. She knew how to put a fire under them. They spent their days guarding the pet cemetery.

"And you were the one showing up again and again doing suspicious things. No wonder they hounded you. How could she explain your digging up graves in the middle of the night?"

"On the other hand, she knew that the dog was poisoned. If I ate it, I would die. Why wouldn't that be fine with her? Then her problem would be solved. She must've known I wouldn't eat it."

"Ah, the boys wouldn't have known that."

"Ok. But why was Merriweather obsessed with me eating dead pets?"

Fritz said, "The human mind is a great mystery. Maybe she

cracked. Maybe she didn't like people desecrating pet graves. Maybe she was covering up some wider scheme. Maybe you were about to blow things wide open."

"Or all of the above."

Fritz spelled it out. If she's judged criminally insane, she wouldn't go to prison but to a hospital. Meanwhile the investigation into the poisoning would peter out. Whatever she was doing, maybe with co-conspirators, wouldn't be discovered. In a short time, her mental state would improve, and she'd be let out.

He went on, "It's hard to believe that she was putting on an act. She was about to kill anyone in her way. She was over the edge."

"The simple explanation might be the right one. She got obsessed, cracked, and set out to kill me."

"Not a pleasant thought Jack. Not a pleasant thought."

I pointed out that it was hard to chart a course from here. Possibilities were all over the map.

Fritz said, "Right now you have to see what Lou and Pete do. They know much more about Merriweather than we do."

Fritz gave me my next step. Get close to them and pick their brains.

"Sounds like fun. Sounds like slim pickin's. I'm glad you're doing it rather than me. After you pick their brains, don't eat them. It'll make your color worse."

53

JOHNNY O'S BLUES

The hero's dinner with Julie seemed to do the trick. Soften up the boys and get them talking. I thought that Julie could have another friendly dinner. I could tap them for what they were now thinking. I didn't know if Julie would go along with it. Through all of this, Julie was my staff. I stopped by the hotel to pick up a bite. A convention had one of those afternoon receptions. After a short while, pastries were left on the trays. I scored some of those little cream puffs with the chocolate dabble on top. They also had little slivers of white cake with raspberry jam between the layers. Quite a find.

I had to go to the riverbank where Johnny had his tent. I knew that he must be worked up about being the poster boy on the fence. He was sitting under his tree. His torso was so long that he was nearly eye level with me while sitting down. He wasn't happy to see me. I knew I couldn't smooth things over but it was important to let some of the pressure out of the tea kettle. Let him blow off some steam.

"What're you doing here?"

"Don't worry Johnny O, I'm not going to ask you to go on another job."

"Any more jobs and I'll end up in prison. I can't walk down the street without being stared at."

"I'd blame the media, but I know I'm responsible for setting the disaster up."

"Carrying that shovel and pole down the street wasn't smart. Somebody reported seeing me with that shovel and pole near the cemetery. A reporter showed up here to get my side of the story. There was no story."

Johnny wasn't quick witted. A reporter could easily stump him. I could come up with a smartass response like, "I'm carrying this shovel because I'm going to dig for worms. I'm going fishing. I'm carrying it in the pet cemetery because that's where the best worms are." Johnny just got embarrassed.

"I don't want people showing up here. What if they wreck my tent or steal my stuff?"

I understood that Johnny didn't want to be a celebrity. He wanted to be left alone. All the lights that were on him might just make him move on. Why put up with this attack on his dignity? I told him that if he decided to pack up and hit the road, I'd help him. I was talking out of my hat in order to save face and make him feel better. Since Arbuckle stiffed me, I'd no money to spare.

"And then those two nosy cops showed up."

"What did they want?"

"They wanted to know what I was doing with the shovel and pole near the cemetery."

"What did you tell them?"

"I told them that I was meeting some other friends and we were going to head out to do something."

"Didn't they ask what?"

"Sure, and I told them that it was a free country and it was none of their business."

"I guess that stopped them."

"Lucky I told them that because they then said that they knew of other people walking near the cemetery with shovels. The one that does most of the talking said that one of those other people was you."

My blood ran cold.

"Thanks for the heads-up Johnny. They haven't gotten around to me yet, and I'm glad to know they're out for me."

"Don't thank me. If I could end this thing by telling them what I know about you, I would say it right away."

I said again that I'd like to help him. "What about the money for doing community service?" I said I'd catch up with him as soon as I could. On my way to Julie's, I thought I would tell her that I had to give the Polaroid camera back to Narcissa so I couldn't take a picture of my big dinner. By now, she wouldn't have believed me if I greeted her with leftovers.

I showed Julie the newspaper and how the cops were acting like I was a criminal again. She said that it won't take them long to figure out that spotting you with a shovel near the cemetery was on the same night that you were late for the heroes' dinner. I hadn't thought of that. Things had been happening fast. I didn't have time to put things together.

"I'd like to have another dinner for the boys to find out what they're up to."

"They wouldn't fall for it in a minute. They might use the dinner to level all sorts of charges against you."

Hum. They might come to the dinner to ambush me. That'd be bad. I asked her for help.

"Well Julie, I need a different plan to find out what they're up to. Got any ideas?"

"You could try telling them the truth."

"Whenever I tell them the truth, they blow it off. It doesn't faze them. To them only what they already think matters."

"If they thought you're telling the truth, they'd believe it."

"Are you saying that they usually think I'm lying?"

"They act that way."

I wouldn't say they thought I was lying. I'm more clever than that. I'm indirect. I pad what I say. I beat around the bush. I came back with, "Maybe they are just stubborn. They won't give up their own version of things. They don't want to lose ego points."

"In that case, there isn't much you can do."

We went on that way for a while. One way or another, I did need to find out what they were doing. Level with them in an "in all sincerity speech?" That's not a way to bring it off. Julie then lit that miserable candle. There were the morsels. We swallowed them. I heard mine echo when it hit the bottom of my stomach. I began having a headache. Living on vapors made me lightheaded. I decided to go home and get some shuteye. Sometimes if you sleep on a problem, a new day will bring something to light.

54

RUFUS

I awoke just as tired as when I went to bed. Nothing like waking up to those damn garbage trucks banging the dumpster lids. Did they make a racket. Stan was also banging pots and pans below. Pots and pans? I felt mossy and sluggish but my ears perked up. He might be making breakfast. I casually went downstairs.

"Knock. Knock."

"Who's there?"

"Atilla."

"Atilla who?"

"Atilla the Hun-gry."

"Very funny Jack. Come on in."

I could tell he'd a lot on his mind. He began with that homicidal maniac who put the axe in my door.

"What about her?"

"I've seen her before."

"Here?"

"No, at that hospital place Elysian Fields. Her loony father was staying there. She was a regular fixture in his room."

I said cleverly, "The mango doesn't fall far from the tree." It was early morning, so my wit was still sharp. Stan pretended not to hear what I said.

"Oh sure, he now lives on the grounds of that pet cemetery

that you can't stay away from."

At that moment, I had one of those "Ah. Ha!" experiences. Was her father a player in all this?

After smoking a few cigarettes and drinking a couple of cups of black coffee, I was fully present. Stan cooked up some fatty bacon and floated some eggs in the grease. We finished off with a couple Danishes hiding under a thick layer of sugar. I thanked Stan for the food and information. He added,

"He was here for Dyngus Day. He came late like you did. He couldn't walk so well. A couple of aides carried him up the steps. He sat in his wheelchair in the corner and hardly said a word. He was staring at you when you came in."

"That's good info Stan."

"I think he was sizing you up."

I told Stan that I knew nothing about the guy and asked if it looked like he was stalking me.

"I don't think so. He can't stalk so well in that wheelchair. I wanted you to know all of this so you can watch out."

I felt embarrassed that I'd little to report to Stan. I told him that Prosecutor Jackson was getting ready for another court hearing. She and the cops were supposed to look into the dog poisonings. The charges against Merriweather would grow.

"Look out for that guy in court. He's very old and square looking. Even his head is square with a full brush of white hair."

I told Stan I'd keep my eyes open. I decided to follow up Stan's lead and head to Elysian Fields. I asked at the desk for a resident named "Merriweather." They said that he'd been released some months ago. I asked what room he stayed in. I went down the hall to it. Sure enough, it was the room with Blockman's bag of botulism-ruined dog food outside the sliding glass door. I popped in on Fanny Blockman.

"I was out here on another matter. I thought I'd stop by and say hello."

"I'm glad you did Mr. de Loosher. I've been reading about Miss Merriweather's attempt to shoot you."

I let her in on some information. Miss Merriweather was in on killing Muffin.

"That's hard to believe. She was such a nice young lady always visiting her father Rufus when he stayed here."

I mentioned what Lou and Pete said about her being very strong.

"She was a body builder. She sauntered around like an animal before an attack. But she was sweet as a kitten. She was so strong she could lift Rufus while he was in his wheelchair."

"Amazing. Sounds like she was showing off."

"She was capable of handling Rufus. He became stable with medications. They sent him home with her."

"After Lilly died from that dog attack, did you give your dog food to Rufus?"

"I did. He got dog food from a number of residents. He said he had big dogs at home."

Another connection was in place. There were other bags of dog food, probably just as bad. It's a short step. A very short step for Rufus to realize its deadliness, get the idea for the poisonings, and feed it to up and coming residents of his cemetery. I said goodbye to Fanny and told her I'd bring her any new developments.

When I got back to town, I was pulled over by the boys. As I rolled down the window, Lou said,

"We're getting the goods on you Jack. After reading about your shovel brigade, we went back to Heaven's Rest. Seven more graves had been dug up."

"Why would you think I'd anything to do with it?"

"You and that Indian fella were I.D.ed with shovels."

"There's no law against carrying a shovel."

"It fits your MO."

"What's that?"

"The graves dug up were all fresh. No old graves were dug up. The fresh ones were just the sort that your syndicate of cannibals likes."

I didn't want to repeat the business of what a cannibal is, so I tried to change the subject.

"Is there some traffic violation?"

"Your parking lights are out."

I got out of the car to look. They were on.

"Oh, they must've just come on," Lou said.

That called for a little sarcasm.

"The car fixed itself. I've got the only self-healing car. You guys are barking up the wrong tree. I told you guys when all of this started that I'd clue you in. I now know more. Let's get together to share notes. We're on the same side. I can use your help."

The offer caught Lou off guard. We agreed to meet at the diner later that afternoon.

55

LEVELING WITH THE BOYS

I had to think about how much I wanted to tell the boys. I wanted them off my back. With the crazy background of this case, who knows how the stories might snake around? Who knows what they would come up with next? Fritz was sober about these things. I stopped at the museum to fill him in. He was working with the canaries. I always liked canaries. I liked the look of them. I liked their song. I told this to Fritz.

"Yes Jack-man, I love working with canaries. They sing like no other bird. People used to keep canaries as pets. Not so much anymore."

"Talk about singing. The cops are singing the 'Let's Prosecute Jack' song. One day they're going to push me too far."

"Like right into a prison cell. What do they have on you?" he asked.

"They discovered the seven disturbed graves. They're pointing the finger at us. Lou is still accusing us of 'diabolical cannibalism.'"

"I was thinking, Jack, if Prosecutor Jackson exhumes the graves, the cops will learn from their own people that the dogs were poisoned."

I said that would help. I told him that Julie wanted me to tell Lou and Pete the truth. She thought the boys would then drop the cannibalism thing. On the downside, they had me for digging up graves and carving samples from the dogs.

"It's up to Jackson."

"Who would she pick to prosecute? The dog poisoner or we who flush out crime?"

"Put that way, I vote for the poisoners. I guess you have second thoughts about your plan Jack."

On my way to the diner, I saw a street vendor selling flowers. Six dollars a dozen. I began to feel a little romantic. Julie had a heart of gold. I wanted to soften her up a bit. I managed to buy one carnation for fifty cents. The soup kitchen was right around the corner. I scored a tub of buttered popcorn. I told them to have a heavy thumb pressing the butter-button. They always put the popcorn out in the afternoon. I ate it on the way to the diner.

Fortunately, no one had identified Mabel with a shovel that night. She was nervous anyway about having the cops there. I gave her Julie's carnation. That softened her a little. Of course, I didn't tell her, "Mabel, here, you can have Julie's carnation." Sometimes it's better to say less. There're fewer hurt feelings. Besides, Mabel never liked the cops hitting her up for free coffee and donuts. I ordered some black coffee, lit up a cigarette, and sat down with the boys.

"Now guys what do you have on Merriweather?"

"You go first Jack. We want to hear what you have to say for yourself."

"Ok, I'll go first. I was supposed to find out what happened to that little dog Muffin— the one found mutilated at the top of a tree."

Lou said, "We wondered how it happened too. We thought, 'Who would do such a weird thing? Oh yeah, it must've been Jack the shamus.'"

"Very funny. Just like you guys to think that someone's paying me to investigate myself."

Pete said, "You've done stranger things in the past."

"I was following a lead that told me the dog was poisoned."

"How could a poisoned dog climb a tree? How can any dog climb a tree?" Lou asked.

"That was what I tried to find out. How it got up there."

"Sounds crazy Jack. When looking into a case, you sure use your imagination. Ha. Ha."

I said, "Try to be serious guys." I told them my buddy at a lab said a sample of the dog revealed the poison. I mentioned that I suspected rat poison but it turned out to be botulism.

"It's in food, isn't it?" Lou asked.

"Yeah, most likely poisoned dog food. I set out to dig up the dog and get a sample. You guys came along and accused me of eating dead dog."

"Now wait a minute Jack. You said the dead dog in that Chinese carton wasn't poor little Muffin. If we thought it was poor little Muffin, we would've run you in right then and there."

"I lied. Muffin died from bad dog food. To make a long story short, I came to believe that other dogs were being poisoned to sell their owners cemetery plots. The short of it is that I tried to get samples and test the results."

Pete said, "That's a story shamus Jack. We heard you say most of this before. What's new? What're you leveling with us about? Who is supposed to be poisoning the dogs? It can't be Merriweather. She loves dead dogs. She protects their little dead bodies. She counsels grieving owners. They miss their cute little pets. The part of the story you left out is about your syndicate and most of the crimes you committed."

I said, "I figured that I couldn't let you guys in on my suspicions. You wouldn't believe me. You know Merriweather wouldn't want police looking into the graves."

"You got that right." Pete said. "She got us to stake out the cemetery to keep the likes of you away from the graves. She installed that surveillance camera. She was fanatical. Every time we were on a break or attending to official business, she'd call the station and ask where we were. She hounded us. We were hardly able to take enough time to eat. We watched those graves like a hawk."

"It's straight fiction that Merriweather was protecting dead dogs."

"We have evidence Jack," Lou said.

"Like what?"

"Merriweather had us watch the graves and lo and behold there you were with your shovels and gang. You were desecrating the remains of that poor little dog and eagle and other little dogs and maybe even eating them."

Lou went on. "When we told her what was going on, she flew into a rage. She said to stop them at all costs. She brought up that you guys were ghouls."

"I thought you guys made that one up."

"Look in the mirror Jack. You need a more alive look. Try a little mortician's makeup in the morning."

Lou said, "That woman was a bulldog about protecting the little doggie graves from ghouls. Our order was to stop the ghouls from getting to the graves. If she was responsible for anything, it was keeping the sanctity of the grave."

Pete said, "I think you have the story wrong Jack. Merriweather doesn't care about money. She finds it horrible that anyone raids graves in the middle of the night. Why did you always show up in the dark after the place was closed?"

I said, "I thought, maybe mistakenly, that the owners would never let the dogs be tested. Arbuckle threw a two-hour fit, with tears, screaming, and all, after you guys snitched on me."

"You deserved it," Pete said. "You were working for her. Try respecting her little doggy's body. We thought that maybe she'd fire you."

"Well, I thought I would level with you guys. Give you a heads up. Prosecutor Jackson might ask you to look into the poisonings."

Lou replied, "For all we know right now, you and your ring were digging up fresh treats for yourselves the other night.

Ordinary citizens gave us eyewitness reports of your crew. Your people weren't regular people. As motley as a group of grave robbers could be. Where did you find those people? Did you run a ghouls job ad in the paper?"

"How stupid can your gang be? Carrying shovels and flashlights around the cemetery," Pete added.

After all their wild accusations, I couldn't resist taking a shot at them.

"My gang was on its way to a shovel party. If you go to a shovel party at night, you need a flashlight. Besides I was with you guys celebrating your arrest of Merriweather."

Right away Lou caught the fact that I slipped up. He accused me of holding the hero's dinner to keep them from catching me and cracking the case.

I countered with, "Guys, I was at the dinner with you."

"Only after you opened and desecrated seven fresh graves. And they were all of little dogs."

Pete added, "Those darling, cute dogs deserved better."

"Think guys. Why would I want to eat poisoned dog? I'd be poisoned too. What do you think Lou, that we're going to sell it on the open market?"

"You wouldn't care if other dead dog gourmets died; you would've gotten your money."

I said suppose I sold decaying dog, I wouldn't sell poisoned dog. I'd have integrity. I would've made sure that it wasn't poisoned.

Pete replayed his tape loop. "You're one to talk about integrity Jack. You look bad. You're almost a cadaver yourself. You're always white as a sheet. What are you some kind of "white-blooded" American?"

Our meeting had gotten out of hand, and I realized, end it before it turns into saying things that they'd never forget or forgive.

"Ok guys, I want you to look into all of this. You'll find the poisoning is true and that my friends aren't a gang. Nobody traffics in little dog parts. You look into that too."

"That is what we've been doing Jack. We'll get you. That Merriweather woman might be strong. She might be violent. But she's right on target that you shouldn't desecrate graves of poor little dogs. The prosecutor had second thoughts about the charges against Merriweather after we explained all of what was going on with the graves."

56

KICKED WHEN DOWN

Holy cripe, they'd already talked to Jackson and defended Merriweather against me! I hadn't counted on that. I had to check in with Jackson to gauge her attitude and learn her plans. On my way, I needed an energy boost. I was worn out from that conversation with Lou and Pete. I slugged down a couple of cans of Coke and ate one of those pieces of cherry pie that comes in its own wrapper.

When I entered Jackson's office, she was glad to see me. She said that we needed to clear up some things. I said that's why I was there.

"Merriweather's attorney told me that her client didn't know anything about poisoning dogs to sell plots. The police told her that grave robbers were working the cemetery. She had the police stake out the fresh graves. The police said they almost caught you and your friends in the act, more than once. A lot of this is hard to explain."

I gave her my side of things that I was taking samples to prove poisoning. Merriweather with policemen Lou Girth and Pete Robusta came up with the ghoul business. Those guys must've been born on Halloween. Besides, if anyone had eaten the dog samples, they would've been dead from botulism."

Jackson then said, "We are going to exhume the seven graves that your lab guy tested. If your results are right, I will add the poisoning charge to the others against Merriweather. In addition, officers Girth and Robusta said they are willing to defend Merriweather against you. We'll hold a meeting in my office with you and the officers to sort out how to proceed."

Right away I protested. I'd already been fined and given community service at the cemetery. The only additional charge was the thin case that I was outside the cemetery with a shovel the night that the Magnificent Seven did their work.

Jackson explained that the problem was that I came to her with results from illegal samples of dogs.

"Wouldn't I be a friend of the court helping bring Merriweather to justice?"

"We'll see what the officers say."

I knew I needed the public defender again, but I couldn't get one because no charges had been filed against me. I slinked over to Julie's needing some tender love and care. I had no such luck. She started up right away.

"Look what the cat dragged in."

"Why the abuse Julie?"

"Lou and Pete have been following you around and told me what you've been eating."

"You don't believe that dog business?"

"No. They said you spend all day scrounging around for junk food."

"Why didn't they tell you about the big healthy dinners I've been eating?"

"I don't know what to believe about that. They didn't catch you in that act. They said they caught you with all of that junk food."

I began to suspect that Julie asked the boys to tail me and report what I'd been eating. Anger began to well up.

"What I eat is nourishing to me. They wouldn't sell it if it wasn't supposed to be eaten."

That was the thinnest excuse I ever came up with about food. If people liked to eat cardboard, they would sell it in five flavors. I was embarrassed. She trapped me.

"You need to see that doctor right away. You've got a screw loose," as she pointed to her head.

I tried to turn it around. "Every time you are having trouble with your weight, my weight becomes the issue. You're projecting."

"I care about you Jack de Looshen. You need to see a doctor to put you on a better course. Lou and Pete said in all sincerity that word on the street was that you've been eating parts of exhumed pets."

"Are the pet parts deep fried or dripping with sugar? They'd better be or I wouldn't touch them. Why would you even bring that one up? How did the word get onto the street? You know who gave the street that rumor. The boys and wildly crazy Meadowlark Merriweather. That nut feeds on what Lou and Pete tell her. They're willing to think the worst especially about me."

We were in for a long night. I needed to break away. I made up some story that I was taking Lou and Pete out for a bite to explain they had it all wrong. I didn't sound convincing. I had to get out of there. She softened a bit. At least I didn't have to stay to face that damned candle and morsel.

57

JACKSON'S MEETING

I had to calm down. I went for a walk. I kept looking over my shoulder to see if Lou and Pete were following me. They're so bad at tailing someone. How did I miss them taking down what I'd been eating lately? Julie must've hit their soft spot to get them to help her. The soft spot was their stomachs. She probably filled those stomachs with more of the goodies she'd hidden from me. As I walked, I thought about the upcoming meeting with Jackson. Much hinged on that meeting.

After walking for an hour, I began to feel light-headed. That one was on Julie since she'd been starving me ever since she went on that diet. As I cleared the top step leading to my door, I saw the big scar left by the axe. I thought, there's a guide to finding my place. I'd just say, "Go up to the unit with the big axe scar on the door."

I had a couple of those Polish pastries. They were beyond their prime, but they filled the void so I could get to sleep. I mulled over what might be brought up at the meeting. I was in for a restless night. I knew pretty much what Jackson and the boys would say. So, as I tossed and turned and worked hard to get to sleep, I loaded up with answers to just about any question that might come up.

Preparation breeds confidence. By morning, I was loaded for bear. In all, Jackson seemed like a good egg. She tried to be fair. I kept reminding myself that she had a stake in this game because of her lost eagle. Anybody who loses an eagle has a stake in the game.

I was already awake when the alarm went off. I was a wreck. They wanted me to look bad. I did look bad. Let's hear some more about how bad I look. I won't disappoint them. Let's talk about that for half an hour before we talk about the case. I took a look in the mirror. I had a sort of moldy look. Maybe that's an improvement over pale white? I was ready for the wise cracks. I skipped the diner and went straight to the courthouse.

When I entered Jackson's office, she was business-like; she wanted to get it over with.

"I confirmed that six of the recent dogs in the cemetery died from botulism. The question is who did it? I agree with you Mr. de Loosher. Merriweather is the likely suspect."

Lou then said, "I don't think that she'd be involved in that. There could've been a bad batch of dog food out there and the owners killed their own dogs. Of course, they didn't know the food was bad."

I countered, "It was the same strain of botulism that killed all the dogs. It had to be more than coincidence. All of the dogs were tiny and chubby with, I'll bet, sentimental old ladies as owners."

Jackson then said, "That sounds right. If there was a lot of bad food out there, you wouldn't expect it to be only killing the tiny dogs."

Pete responded, "Maybe there're dozens of dead dogs out there. Maybe there's a crisis from the poisoning. The large old ladies may be the only ones to spend the money on a pet cemetery. Lou and I suspect that the dogs may have been poisoned after they were buried."

"How so?" I asked.

"Suppose the syndicate of dog ghouls dug up the graves, took the choice parts to sell or eat, and poisoned what was left."

I asked, “How in the world can you poison a dead dog?” Lou replied, “Jack’s been saying that his gang wouldn’t eat poisoned dog. Sure, they wouldn’t. But how do we know that the chunks they tested weren’t tampered with?”

Jackson reacted, “There is a chain of evidence problem. My people only tested the dogs after your group exhumed the dogs. We’d have to trust your people Jack.”

This caught me totally off guard. I was scrambling to find an answer. They blindsided me.

“I can’t say, ‘trust’ me, since you all are raising doubt about trusting me. What about science?”

Lou asked, “What science Jack?”

Pete seconded, “Yeah, what science?

“Er, when botulism goes through the body killing somebody, it’s in all the tissues. If somebody injects botulism in a dead dog, the poison would be in one place. There’d be no pumping heart to send it around.”

I liked my answer. I was quick on my feet. Jackson thought the answer worth looking into. She phoned the police lab to get someone to come up to her office to give an opinion.

We waited. It seemed forever. The boys weren’t their jolly old wiseacre selves. Jackson acted like she was wasting time. Then in pops Narcissa. We put the question to her. She said,

“Botulism kills fast. Te, he, he, he. Te, he, he, he. It wouldn’t be uniformly in every tissue. On the other hand, you couldn’t poison a dead dog without it being superficially on the skin or concentrated at a local site.”

“I was right. So, you can trust what I said.”

The boys were unhappy. They tried for a comeback.

“But, but Prosecutor Jackson, they could have switched dogs. They could have put poisoned ones into the graves.”

I said, “Look Lou, if we were up to that, we would have no reason to dig dogs up. We would just use the unpoisoned ones. They’re more tasty anyway.”

Jackson didn’t like my answer.

"Quit the sarcasm Mr. de Loosher."

Pete said, "If they weren't poisoned, they would still be alive. They would be cutting up live dogs."

Jackson disagreed. "That doesn't follow Officer Robusta."

I'd pretty well convinced Jackson that no further action was necessary on the ghoul charges. It happened just in time because Narcissa was about to start circling the room. I was relieved that the boys couldn't finger Narcissa as one of the grave robbers. That would've opened up a whole new can of worms.

58

MAYHEM IN COURT

We had one more court appearance with the modified charges against Merriweather. I knew it'd be a circus. I was glad Stan gave me a heads up about Rufus. Just as we were to get started, there was some rustling in the back of the room followed by grunts. They became louder and louder. The loud grunts were chilling. 'UMAUGH! UMAUGH!" We all turned around. There was the big guy in the wheelchair with the square head full of white hair. The judge warned him about being quiet or he'd be removed. He looked fearsome. We were glad he was in the wheelchair. He couldn't easily move in on us.

Merriweather's attorney was ready for Jackson. Her client pleaded innocent to the new charge of poisoning dogs to sell plots. Then this pounding sound pierced the room. The old man was pounding his cane on the floor creating a loud echo. BLAM! BLAM! BLAM! The judge ordered him removed. All of this agitated Meadowlark. She looked like she was about to burst. Fortunately, she didn't see me because I was standing next to Lou Girth and couldn't be seen. His belly shielded me from her view.

Merriweather's attorney wanted the poisoning charge dismissed.

"Your honor, they've no evidence to connect my client to such a conspiracy. In fact, two fine police officers have something to say."

Lou started. "Yes your honor, we've something to say about those charges."

The judge made circles with his hands signaling that he wanted them to get on with it. The boys had a prepared statement.

"You're honor, we want to say that Miss Merriweather cares about dead dogs and would do nothing to harm them. You remember what happened in court. When she saw Jack de Loosher, she flew into a rage and accused him of eating dead little dogs. She reacted not for her own safety but in defense of those poor defenseless animals."

Pete followed with, "We have been working this case for some time, and always, Miss Merriweather put the dead dogs first."

Lou said, "We nearly died when Miss Merriweather was about to unload her big hand gun, her cannon, on us. We knew she liked us. No matter. She was single-minded. She was going to get the grave robber who didn't respect anything sacred."

I interjected, "Your honor, it isn't my fault that Miss Merriweather was homicidal. Who filled her mind with the tripe about eating dead dog? The rumor spreaders are standing right there." I pointed to Lou and Pete.

Merriweather went ballistic. She turned, charged, and tried to get around Lou. His belly prevented her from getting a clean swipe at me. She went off balance when she lunged for my throat. It took Lou, Pete, and a bailiff to hold her back. She was removed from the court.

The judge let the prosecution proceed with the charge about dog poisonings. Lou and Pete were restless and unhappy. I was relieved. After all of this, the little dogs were about to receive some justice. Someone would account for the crime. It was now up to the prosecutor and police to build the case. Because Merriweather was a danger to society, bail was denied. Actually, she didn't seem a danger to anyone but me.

59

MORE QUESTIONS

Trials take a long time to organize. Six months later, the trial was held. It turned into one big fat disappointment. Lou and Pete were less than enthusiastic about connecting Merriweather to the poisonings. Jackson proved that the seven dogs, which included Muffin, were poisoned. The problem was that Merriweather's actions before and after the death of Muffin weren't looked into.

The boys were assigned to do the investigating. They spent a lot of time on assignment or on official business. You could see them around town at their usual haunts. The prosecutor just didn't have the right manpower to make the case. No search warrant was issued for Merriweather's home to find the tainted dog food or list of targets. Since I wasn't being paid, I let the matter drop. The jury found Merriweather not guilty of that charge.

I talked to Julie about the verdict, and she agreed with the jury. There was no direct evidence that Merriweather did any poisoning. She benefitted from the poisonings. Jackson proved that she sold more plots. Julie said that maybe Merriweather was telling the truth. She wanted to kill me just for digging around in the cemetery. Julie holds to that version of the story. To me, that seemed a stretch. I still think that Meadowlark and Rufus planned the whole scam together.

You never know when you bring out others murderous instincts. I still have nightmares about running into a stranger who's driven to kill me from out of the blue. I've been at this business for a long time, and I've yet to figure out what tips some people over the edge.

If Merriweather didn't know about the poisonings, then who did it? Julie thought that Rufus fits the bill. He was the friend of Fanny Blockman that she gave her dog food. On Julie's scenario, Rufus identified the little dogs through the pet program at Elysian Fields and maybe elsewhere. There were many rectangular older ladies there. He stalked the dogs, fed them the poison, and their owners bought plots. To me, the guy grunting and pounding in court didn't seem to have the ability to do all of that.

Julie thinks Meadowlark Merriweather didn't know what Rufus was doing. She just sold the plots and managed the cemetery. Could be. But the police didn't investigate Rufus. He's now in his wheelchair sitting on his porch overlooking the pet cemetery. His square head of thick white hair stands out even way up there on the hill. I checked Heaven's Rest every now and then. There were no new strings of tiny dog graves.

The prosecution also wanted to call Albion Arbuckle to testify. They couldn't find her. It was as if she vanished from the planet. She's back on that space ship, sagging it, going who knows where. Probably some place very dusty. I checked obits from area newspapers for some time. No Arbuckle. I decided not to spend more time finding her. In court, they couldn't prove that I was even hired to investigate the case of Muffin. For all they knew, my client Arbuckle may never have existed.

I was glad that Jackson didn't come right out and accuse me of abusing Alfie's remains. Why would she even think that? Well, the boys can be persuasive. She was suspicious of just what my game was. The boys in blue tried out all sorts of wild stories on her. Just to fuel her suspicions, whenever they had the chance.

The saving grace was that Merriweather was declared a danger. I think she was close to being criminally insane. The cops set up the right verdict. Lou and Pete had put their lives on the line. So they didn't back off saying Merriweather was a danger to society. Nevertheless, they still insisted that she respected dead dogs. She's currently in a hospital. I hoped that whenever the staff would be tempted to release her, they'd show her my picture. That'd convince them that she was still a danger to my part of the public.

60

WHAT DID HAPPEN?

As you can tell, I survived beyond the trial. Lived to tell the tale so to speak. I added some fruits and vegetables to my diet. I especially like strawberry jam and ketchup. Just kidding. Whenever I use that joke, no one laughs. Do you think it's funny that nobody laughs? I do. It's a riot. Julie went on and off diets on a regular basis. We've been together long enough for me to negotiate that minefield. She did lose and keep off a few pounds. I'm back to snacking at her place.

One day I deep-sixed the scale that started all the trouble. Nasty scale. Nasty scale. Right into the river. I don't know if I look any better, as they say, more alive. Everyone got in the habit of telling me how bad I looked. I don't think they look very carefully any more. I'm skinny as ever. They tell me I look older. I don't think they intend that as a compliment.

I kept that doctor's appointment. Just like always, he didn't really want to see me. He tried to look the other way. Try to give a physical to someone while trying to look the other way. He did write a few prescriptions. I took the pills but nothing, regarding how I was feeling, changed for the better. Julie was satisfied that I wasn't going to die soon.

All the publicity about the trial helped business. I became the dangerous private investigator into crimes against pets. I suppose I carried that spark of danger just as any cannibal would. I specialized in small dogs, especially the chubby ones. May as well cash in on my fame and expertise.

Andre the pet groomer still reeks of pet perfumes. He never did get those front teeth fixed. Jungle Tom continues to walk in an envelope of gorilla essence lisping away on matters where he has an inside track. Birdman Fritz started a shelter for injured birds. His house is full of them. More cages to clean. I can as always count on Mabel for stale donuts. Narcissa still does great work and is always a livewire when I visit. Johnny O moved on. I still feel bad that I added to his troubles and couldn't help him more. If I could find him, I'd set things right. I have to admit, though, I haven't been looking for him.

Now you are up to date on the whole crew. The case of Muffin taught me again about really investigating something. When I really checked things out, I found out that most of what happened was in a big world of things I didn't know. Many were things I could never know. Many were things that nobody could know. They were beyond reach. For all we knew, some things just appeared out of nowhere and then disappeared into somewhere.

No one experienced what actually happened to Muffin. Don't get me wrong, other people helped fill in some blanks but that raised more questions than I cared to deal with. Maybe I'm sounding dramatic. Maybe I'm not. Who knows? Nobody, that's who. Most everything that happened with that dog is still a mystery.

That doesn't stop me from having my take on things. I'm convinced about what happened to Muffin. Since I looked into it, mine is the best story. Just ask me. No one else who cares at all about the case agrees with my version of the story. I keep getting push-back. It'd be nice if Julie agreed with more of it. I had to admit something to her. The whole story might not be true. Maybe a lot of it just couldn't be. Did Albion Arbuckle want to know what happened to her dog? Did Muffin die of other causes? Did the lawnmower mutilate the dog? Was there a jaguar in the park? Did Merriweather know about the poisoning? Was Rufus the real criminal? I could go on and on. I peeled back a few layers for poor little Muffin's sake— that poor little angel of a victim. I'm telling the truth, really. I know I keep saying that. We have no God's eye view. We only pretend that it is out there to find.

CPSIA information can be obtained
at www.ICGtesting.com
Printed in the USA
FFHW021344221019
55666626-61501FF

9 781977 212696